Repent

K-9 Mystery Series

Bev Pettersen

Published by Bev Pettersen, 2021.

Westerhall Books

Hard Cover Print ISBN: 978-1-987835-26-7

For my dad. Thanks for always being there.

CHAPTER ONE

The pigs were squealing again.

Billy Tanner pressed his head between his knees and edged further against the wall, desperate to block their sounds. Steel shackles had rubbed his skin raw but he'd grown accustomed to the pain, and to the precise length of his ankle chain.

He knew every inch of this abandoned horse stall: the eight spikes in each thick plank, the two feet of wire mesh that covered the gap below the ceiling, and how his steel tether stopped him exactly seven inches from the door.

He hadn't been the only one thrust in here. A bloody fingernail protruded from beneath a splinter in the wood. At first the sight had freaked him out. Now it was merely part of his prison. At least that poor soul—a woman judging by the color and elegant shape of the nail—hadn't given up. She'd tried to escape, even though prying out the heavy studs was impossible. Billy had learned that by his second day. Their captor had been very thorough with stall reinforcement.

And the surveillance camera in the corner always kept a vigilant eye. Of course when the pigs were squealing for food, like now, it meant his captor wasn't watching the camera.

Billy lurched to his feet, seizing the opportunity. His chain clinked as he shuffled across the stained wood to the far wall.

"Hey, mister," he whispered, shoving his face against the plank and peering through the crack in the boards. "Want me to splash more water through the mesh? It's okay. He's not watching now."

But the naked man curled in the corner of the adjacent stall didn't answer. His only movement was the shudder of skeletal ribs as he pulled in labored breaths.

"You should suck some more on that old bone," Billy said. "Still lots of nutrition there." However, his voice quivered with a despair he couldn't hide. The man was starving to death. And no wonder. He'd never been fed anything but an old soup bone and an occasional drop of water.

It didn't make sense. Billy had been given a bucket of water along with a ration of livestock grain. Admittedly, it wasn't typical people food and his stomach was always cramped with hunger, but at least the grain was top notch, the kind with corn and molasses, the same type they fed the horses at the police stable.

"I can throw over more grain too," Billy said. "But you have to pick it off the floor before *he* comes. Just try to sit up." He gripped the wire mesh, willing the man to answer, no longer worrying about the camera or that talking was strictly against the rules. "Please, mister," he pleaded. "You have to try."

The man didn't seem to hear. He remained curled in a fetal position, his hair long and matted, his back impossibly bony.

Billy pressed a hand to his mouth, fighting his terror. He didn't want to be left alone, not in this horrible place. Having someone else sharing this hellhole—even a mute, broken man—was the only thing that made this torture bearable.

"Please don't give up, mister," he pleaded, ashamed to feel warm tears wetting his cheeks. He couldn't stand to be the only prisoner left. He'd rather die too than be chained in here, alone with nothing but the terrifying whir of a saw. And the squeals of hungry pigs.

CHAPTER TWO

Nikki Drake peered over the vet's shoulder, straining to see the dogs in the therapeutic pool. More precisely, trying to see her dog.

"Gunner's gunshot wound has healed nicely. On the surface." Dr. Martin's voice deepened, his note of caution unmistakable. "Now it's time to try to repair his damaged ligaments. Hydrotherapy is one of the center's many tools. Our underwater treadmill provides a low weight-bearing environment yet helps maintain muscle mass. Some of our K9s have even been able to return to full duty."

Nikki gave a little nod. She didn't care about full duty; she just wanted her best friend to be able to walk again. Without pain, without that bewildered look in his big brown eyes, the type of look that tore at her heart. Besides, Gunner wasn't a police dog. He didn't have to achieve a certain fitness standard. He didn't have to achieve anything.

A black Malinois, clearly not Gunner, vacated the pool, dripping water as two assistants supported him with a full body harness. His ears flattened as he edged forward, stoically responding to their encouragement.

"That particular K9 was struck by a felon's car," Dr. Martin said, following her gaze. "He's just getting back on his feet after surgery. We're hoping he'll be able to return to his handler."

"Is his handler one of those people down on the pool deck?"

"No, only staff works with the animals during rehab. It goes much smoother that way. For patients and people." The vet's gaze dropped to his clipboard, scanning the clinic notes. "As I see you've been warned before."

Nikki crossed her arms, remembering the fiasco when Gunner thought a strange man had stepped too close. He'd leaped off the examination table, determined to protect her at all costs. In the process, he'd fallen and ripped out several stitches and the setback had added weeks to his rehab. She understood that when she was around, Gunner's focus was on her. And his need to protect her. Still, it was hard to see him struggle and not be at his side to give reassurance.

"I just want to help," she said. "And I worry about how he'll react to a pool. Your staff might not understand, you know, what he's been through." She gripped her locked arms, emotion thickening her words.

"We know he almost drowned, before he took a bullet to save you." Dr. Martin shrugged, a little too dismissively for Nikki's liking. "But our techs are experienced in dealing with physical and mental trauma. We also know Gunner is very intelligent and we don't want your subjective emotion transferring to your dog, impeding his progress."

Nikki's mouth tightened but she lowered her arms, trying to portray a more relaxed posture. It was one of the highlights of her day to watch Gunner's morning sessions—always from behind the elevated glass partition—and she didn't want to lose the privilege. But she certainly didn't want to slow his progress.

"I know everyone here is very competent." She forced a smile, determined not to alienate anyone associated with Gunner's care. "And I'm grateful to be able to watch. It's amazing how he's progressed in six weeks. The center is definitely cutting edge."

Dr. Martin's face softened, distracted by the praise, and he went on to talk about how UV filtration helped maintain the purity of the K9 pool—reducing the need for harmful chemicals—and how a heart rate monitor would make sure Gunner wasn't overtaxed. It wasn't necessary to pump the center's merits. In addition to their training, Nikki already knew the K9 center's rehab facility was top notch. She'd studied every feature of the equipment, had researched everything they offered, from their underwater treadmill to laser therapy.

"It's actually unusual that we're treating a dog like Gunner," Dr. Martin added, his head tilting like an inquisitive bird. "We don't usually accept outside animals, other than veterans' service dogs. But Justin Decker advised that you're a private investigator who was consulting for us. A cold case involving a missing teen? That must have been interesting?"

Nikki silently eyed the door that Gunner would soon be entering. She didn't discuss her work with outsiders. And she knew Justin didn't either.

"Well, I'll leave you now," Dr. Martin said, clearing his throat. "I only wanted to warn you to stay back from the window. It won't help Gunner if he sees you."

"I understand." Nikki smiled at the vet now, her gratitude genuine. "Thank you for keeping him safe."

She moved another foot back from the window, earning an approving nod from Dr. Martin before the man exited the room.

On the deck below, the door slid open, revealing a familiar black-and-tan head. She stilled, watching as Gunner entered the room. A harness extended around his belly and he was supported on each side by two handlers. Female handlers, and Nikki blew out a sigh of relief, glad it was Krissy and Karen by his side. Gunner didn't like men, other than a select few, but he'd taken quite nicely to the two techs.

Even with their support, he had a painful limp. But at least his ears were pricked, as if curious about the room and ready for a new challenge. An image popped up of him stuck in a pool, vainly swimming circles with her powerless to help, and she had to force herself to remain well back from the window.

Gunner limped up the ramp and toward the small rectangle of water with Krissy and Karen by his side. They took their time, letting him absorb the solid sides and blinking control panel. He seemed unfazed and steadily moved forward until he was standing on the treadmill, water up to his belly. Maybe they were just standing him on it today, Nikki thought. He probably wasn't ready for movement. They might want her beside him for that.

And then Krissy stepped behind him, pressed a button and Gunner was moving. Careful and cautious, but walking. It didn't look as if he needed much support, just Karen at his side and Krissy behind him, making sure he didn't fall off. Both techs encouraged him with smiles and praise. One of them even glanced toward the viewing room, giving Nikki a quick thumbs-up, knowing she was there.

It was comforting to watch but frustrating to be a bystander. Nikki's good friend, Sonja, kept saying Nikki could help Gunner with positive visualization. But that was difficult. Too often, her images turned to the man who'd shot Gunner, and the emotions that aroused certainly weren't positive.

Her phone vibrated and she eased further back. The glass was soundproof but she didn't want to risk Gunner spotting her arm movement. Right now, he was a model patient, concentrating on the techs' commands and the quicker he healed, the quicker she could take him home. Where she could hug him and love him, and they could both forget about the outside world. Maybe she could even take him away to a cabin somewhere, a dog friendly place where he could enjoy long walks and freedom. Her investigative business could wait.

"Hi, Sonja," she said cheerfully, encouraged by the idea of Gunner padding beneath majestic California oaks, with no need for support and trotting with barely a limp. She'd find an isolated cabin with lots of space and paths with good footing, where he could roll and sniff to his heart's content. Leashes not required.

"How's the patient today?" Sonja asked. "I've been burning some herbs and channeling healing energy."

"Keep it up," Nikki said. "He's on the underwater treadmill now. And doing well." She would never understand Sonja's psychic world but lately had suspended most, if not all, of her disbelief.

"I'm going to stop by the office tomorrow," Nikki added. "And clean up some paperwork. Want to meet for coffee?"

"Definitely," Sonja said. "But I'm calling to warn that there's a woman sitting outside your office door. Poor thing has been camped in the hall for hours, practically tripping people with her cane. I told her you weren't taking new clients, but she refuses to leave."

Nikki paced a circle at the back of the room, mentally reviewing PI acquaintances that might be able to help. The ones she trusted most charged much more than she did. Of course, she was relatively new at the business and Robert had looked after most of their networking. *Robert*. Bile rose in her throat and she swallowed back the bitterness.

"She could call the Taylor Agency," Nikki said, peering back down at Gunner who was stoically moving on the treadmill. "I'll text you the contact information."

Nikki definitely wasn't taking a new case. Didn't have the time or motivation. The center was a two-hour drive from her office so she preferred to stay overnight in the handler's dorm; some afternoons she was allowed to sit outside on the grass with Gunner, depending on his progress. Those moments were precious. And not to be missed.

Frankly, she didn't know if she'd ever be passionate about returning to her typical caseload. Boring surveillance hours, sprinkled with reports to distraught spouses or details on insurance fraud, weren't very fulfilling. If she'd learned anything from her and Gunner's brush with death, it was that life was too short to waste. At the end of the day, she wanted to know that she'd helped people. Not contributed to the slashing of medical benefits or the breakdown of a marriage.

"Here's the number for Taylor," she said, bringing up the information on her phone screen. "I'm forwarding it now."

"But she wants you," Sonja said. "Her name is Mrs. Tanner and she's very insistent."

"She needs to find another investigator. Scott Taylor is good. Much more experienced than me."

"You should talk to Mrs. Tanner first. This is the type of case that drew you into the business. I think you'll want to hear her out."

Nikki stilled. Sonja's voice was oddly grave. Not only that, her friend truly seemed to sense things. Nikki didn't understand the psychic profession but she'd learned never to discount Sonja's advice.

"Okay, what's it about?" Nikki squeezed the phone a little tighter, swept with an odd mixture of hope and dread.

"Her missing grandson."

CHAPTER THREE

"Finally some service!" Mrs. Tanner sniffed, her mouth twisting as if she'd just sucked a lemon. The woman sank onto Nikki's office chair with a long-suffering sigh. "What kind of business are you running? I didn't have to wait nearly this long at the police station."

Nikki remained standing. Once Sonja had mentioned a missing teen, she'd rushed back to meet with this woman. But she wasn't in the habit of accepting unwarranted criticism, especially in her own office. Clearly the woman's attitude was going to make it easier to turn down the case.

"Like my friend told you," Nikki said, "I'm not accepting new cases. But I can make a referral—"

"Why?" Mrs. Tanner snapped. "Are you busy with something more important? Are you looking for another kid? Because I don't know anything more important than that."

Sighing, Nikki pulled out her chair and sat, studying Mrs. Tanner over the wide desk. The woman was blunt, rudely so, but it was impossible to argue with her logic. Watching Gunner's rehab and meeting Justin whenever he had some time filled her hours but that wouldn't satisfy anybody's definition of busy.

Besides, she agreed with the woman. There wasn't anything more important than finding a missing child. She wasn't in this business to make friends. It really shouldn't matter if a client was abrasive.

Clearly Mrs. Tanner liked to speak her mind. And she didn't appear to be a stranger to hard work. Her hands were gnarled and callused, and her frizzy gray hair emphasized a sun-damaged face. She'd leaned heavily on her cane when she had entered Nikki's office, although it was impossible to tell if it was her knees or hips that left her hobbling in pain. Everything about the woman was worn and brittle, except for her deep-set blue eyes which blazed with startling determination.

"The police don't want to help either," Mrs. Tanner said, fixing those accusing blue eyes on Nikki. "They claim Billy's a runaway. But they're wrong. I know my grandson better than anyone else. He's only fourteen, a good kid. He didn't run when *it* happened and he certainly wouldn't run now."

She struggled to catch her breath and Nikki mentally added emphysema to the woman's obvious ailments.

"Now I admit he shouldn't have thrown a Molotov cocktail at that police trailer," Mrs. Tanner said, her voice turning forceful again. "But it was just a horse that was burned. An animal, not a person."

Nikki's eyes widened. Before Mrs. Tanner had sat down, she'd complained about the lack of police service. Now it was obvious why they weren't rushing to find this kid. *Burning a horse.* They must have been devastated to see one of their horses injured in such a deliberate and painful way.

Mrs. Tanner obviously didn't consider hurting an animal to be much of a crime. In fact, she spent the next thirty minutes sitting in the chair, complaining about the disinterest of the police while portraying Billy as the smartest, kindest and most upstanding teenager in California: how he took the bus to school each morning and never skipped a class, how he faithfully was doing court-ordered community service at the police barn, and how he never failed to gather every single chicken egg.

She went on to praise his older brother Jack in the same manner, glossing over the fact that he'd been picked up last year for running with a gang, and that Child Protective Services had been involved. Mrs. Tanner's strong opinions might be irritating, but she was obviously loyal to her two grandsons.

Nikki leaned further back in her chair. The Taylor Agency would not be a good fit for this woman. They probably wouldn't give her the time of day. It was also unlikely Mrs. Tanner could afford their fee. Her gaze drifted to the corner of the room where Gunner used to lie. He was probably in the infrared room now. With a little luck, she'd be able to take him home in another month.

"What are you looking at?" Mrs. Tanner demanded, twisting and spotting Gunner's empty bed. "Do you let dogs in here? I think animals should be kept outside where they belong." Shaking her head, she straightened, her voice rising. "So you see! Billy wouldn't run away."

"I do see," Nikki said. "But at this point you might be wasting your money hiring an investigator. I recommend you wait a few more days. Based on your description"—and she didn't try to keep the coolness from her voice—"a nice kid like Billy will want to come home to help you out."

"But that's my point. If he didn't come home last Saturday, it means he can't. I just w-wish someone would believe m-me."

Nikki swallowed, affected by the quaver in Mrs. Tanner's voice. Nikki hadn't expected that. The woman was wrapped in opinions but for a moment she had shown a vulnerable side. And that moved Nikki far more than the woman's colored opinions.

"Mrs. Tanner," Nikki said, "Billy was doing long hours of community service for maliciously injuring a horse. And his brother has gang contacts. Isn't it possible the police are correct? And that Billy voluntarily left?"

Mrs. Tanner jerked forward, slamming her cane against the floor. "You're just like them! I thought after how long you looked for your sister that you'd understand about family, how it feels when someone disappears. But I was wrong. You're no better than the cops."

She spat out the words as if being compared to the police was the worst thing in the world. And in her experience, maybe it was.

"I take every disappearance seriously," Nikki said. "And I do understand. But your other grandson left home many times before and is definitely streetwise. You stated he was picked up while running with a gang. So there is recurring history of one grandson that could affect the other. And please, if you want me to seriously consider taking your case, you need to stop waving that cane."

Mrs. Tanner's knuckles whitened around the handle. For a moment it seemed as if she'd swing it in Nikki's direction. A moment later though, she hung the cane on the arm of her chair. She harrumphed for several seconds and it was clear apologies were difficult for her.

"It's just that I'm the only one looking out for those two boys," Mrs. Tanner said. "Been that way since their mom died. And this behavior isn't like Billy. You gotta believe me!" Her voice was gathering strength again. "He wouldn't run away. Not Billy. He wouldn't just disappear!"

"Even though he'd been given probation and two hundred hours of community service?" Nikki asked, her voice not ungentle. "Working at a police stable would be tough for anyone but especially for a teen who—"

"Who burned a police horse." Mrs. Tanner gave a grudging nod. "Yes, I know. But he didn't know that animal was in the trailer. He really didn't. And the police might hate him for it, but Billy agreed to the service. He wanted to make up for his mistake. He wouldn't quit. Look, I can pay you. Not right now but I'll pay a little every month. No matter the cost. Please, you gotta find him."

Nikki studied Mrs. Tanner but saw no hint of deceit, only a woman who was accustomed to fighting for everything she owned. Her earlier belligerence was gone, replaced by desperation. The woman truly believed her grandson hadn't chosen to disappear.

But Nikki wasn't ready to take on a new case. Her mind wasn't in the right place. And she could afford to take some time off. Quite likely the kid was sleeping in a park somewhere. Or making more Molotov cocktails.

She rolled a pen between her fingers. She'd intended to call another agency, make sure Mrs. Tanner found someone who'd look after her. It would be challenging though to find a reputable investigator who'd give this case much time, considering the boys' history.

But even if Billy was an unfeeling punk, his grandmother deserved answers. She had sat outside Nikki's office door for five hours. Dressed up in her Sunday best and, judging by the smell of oil, had polished her worn leather shoes. That effort moved Nikki. She remembered how her mother had applied careful makeup before every police meeting. And if Mrs. Tanner's grandson really was in trouble...

Nikki tugged her chair a little closer. "I expect my clients to be totally honest," she said. "It's necessary if we're to have results. So please answer this: Are you sure Billy's not involved with a gang?"

"Absolutely sure." Mrs. Tanner's voice rang with conviction. "Jack was. But not Billy."

"Okay," Nikki said, pulling out her notepad. "I'll need a recent picture. And any other details that can help. Names of friends, hobbies and places he might be hanging out, like a favorite park or mall."

Mrs. Tanner shook her head even as she plucked a clump of papers from her purse. "I have a recent picture and some media clippings, but nothing else. Like I said, Billy's a real country boy. Never slept anywhere but his own bed."

"What about girlfriends? Cell phone number? Instagram or other social media accounts?" Private investigators didn't have many more privileges than citizens but Nikki had cultivated contacts in the various police departments, and much of her legwork was simply knowing who to call. And social media accounts were always a wealth of information.

But Mrs. Tanner gave another headshake. "He didn't have any close friends, not since our neighbors moved away. And he doesn't own a cell phone. The service is too spotty where we live. There's nothing else to tell. Just that he always came home."

Her shoulders sagged. She seemed less combative now. More fragile. "Please find him," she muttered. "Billy means the world to me. He's a sweet boy."

Not so sweet he wouldn't burn a helpless horse, Nikki thought, still fighting her ambivalence. She knew an officer in the city's mounted unit and no doubt Lara also found Billy's actions reprehensible. The police had probably been pushing the kid hard, delighted that the court had assigned community work with their stable. Shoveling shit off the street, cleaning up after their mounted patrols, was no teen's idea of a good time. Especially when it was in view of his peers.

Billy was probably sleeping on a bench somewhere, hoping if he stayed away long enough his problems would disappear. Fourteen-year-olds thought like that. She'd been the same way at his age. Had known every nook and cranny of the city parks, and where the police were most likely to leave her alone.

But Mrs. Tanner was genuinely concerned about her grandson. It probably wouldn't take long to find him, although at the end of the day, Mrs. Tanner might not see Billy through such rose-colored glasses.

Nikki shuffled through the well-worn clippings Mrs. Tanner had placed on the desk and pulled out his picture. Billy was a handsome boy—dark hair, brown eyes and a nice smile—but unfortunately his appearance was similar to a lot of teens. Only his clothing was different. Certainly his hunter plaid shirt differed from the typical tee favored by most kids that age. "Does he always dress like this?" she asked. "Is this what he was wearing last Saturday?"

"Yes, he always wore work shirts and jeans. Billy never cared much about clothes, not like his older brother." Mrs. Tanner brightened. "So you'll look? You'll find him? I have seventy-four dollars in my purse. I'll give you more later, whatever it costs."

"Don't worry." Nikki pulled out a contract, already resolved to give Mrs. Tanner the lowest possible rate. "It probably won't take much time. Just remember that Billy might not be where you expect."

CHAPTER FOUR

"Hi, Nikki," Sgt. Lara McCullough said, striding up to the steel mesh fence while shading her eyes against the lowering sun. She punched in a security code and opened the gate, all the while peering over Nikki's shoulder. "Nice to see you again. Is Justin with you?"

"No," Nikki said. "I'm working my own investigation."

The disappointment on Lara's face was almost comical but Nikki pretended not to notice. And perhaps she hadn't been completely open when she'd called Lara, asking to meet about a case. Still, it was Lara's mistake, to assume that Justin would be with her.

"I don't have much time." Lara spoke a little more crisply now, clicking the gate shut so fast it brushed Nikki's heels. "I just turned Guinness out for a quick roll and need to take him inside for night feed."

"He's a big boy," Nikki said, checking out the thick-necked black horse in the sand paddock. He looked vaguely familiar, big boned with feet the size of dinner plates.

"An Irish Draught," Lara said. She led the way across the parking area, skirting the lone vehicle in the lot, a silver pickup with a bright parking decal. "You saw Guinness at the K9 center working over his fear of dogs. He's good now, the perfect temperament for a police horse. Also a great size for crowd control."

Nikki remembered the occasion, her first visit to the K9 center. It had been obvious then that Lara and Justin shared some history. In fact, at one time Nikki had been rather worried about Justin's friendship with the attractive cop.

"Was Guinness working today?" Nikki asked.

"Yes, we helped with a parade by City Hall. It went well. Patrolling on horseback is much more fun than being in a vehicle. It's nice working with a partner who never talks back." Lara paused, her face shadowing. "I was sorry to hear that your dog took a bullet. Justin said he's coming along well and might even be able to walk normally again."

"Not just walk. He's going to run."

"Let's hope so," Lara said.

Nikki turned away from the skepticism on the woman's face, watching Guinness roll until the faint saddle marks were coated with a layer of sand. "Your horse looks fit. Barely sweating."

"He's in great shape," Lara said proudly. "A gentle giant. Everyone loves him. Except maybe the shoplifter we caught yesterday. It helps to see the street from high up and people respect a horse. It took him a while to get used to barking dogs but now he's the perfect partner."

"Do people ever try to scare him? Hurt him?"

Lara's eyes flashed with indignation. "Over my dead body," she said. "And he's young but not easy to scare. All of our horses are conditioned to stay calm. In chases, fights, all sorts of commotion. Most perps just give up when we get close."

"I can imagine the bond that grows between horse and rider," Nikki said, watching Lara's expression. "Like human and K9. We do what we can to protect them. And want to retaliate if someone hurts them."

Lara's eyes narrowed. "Is this visit about Billy Tanner? His grandmother said she was hiring an investigator. We really don't know why the kid ghosted. Sure, we were angry but we didn't run him off. There are only six mounted officers here and everyone was civil. Admittedly, it took a bit longer for Smitty but even he softened."

"Was it Smitty's horse that Billy burned?"

"Yes. Smitty had hauled back late after reinforcing security at the fairground. He was inside unpacking his tack while Radar was tied in the trailer. A bunch of teens were hanging outside the gate, catcalling and rattling the mesh. At some point it escalated and they tossed a couple Molotov cocktails over the fence. Nothing hit Smitty's truck but one landed in the trailer and burned Radar's back. His screams were horrible. Smitty was as traumatized as the horse."

Nikki pivoted, studying the lot. Two surveillance cameras were mounted beside prominent flood lights, along with a six-foot-high mesh fence topped with three strands of imposing wire. A person would need excellent aim, and a strong arm, to chuck a firebomb over the high fence and through the rear of a trailer.

"Did you replace the horse trailer?" Nikki asked. "Or was it salvageable?"

"No, we don't have the budget and the insurance company deemed it fixable. We had new flooring and a paint job. It's back in service but now we have to park in the patrolled police lot at the corner of Waterloo and Main. It's a hassle, takes an extra half hour at the beginning and end of each day. Luckily City Hall is in riding distance."

"And the lights and cameras were operational that night?"

"Yes, that's why we saw Billy's face. He had to step really close to the fence to make the throw. He came in to the station a couple days later and confessed."

Nikki eyed the thick brush around the fence. They were lucky Billy was caught on camera. It would take time to obtain a copy of the police report through regular channels. But she had a contact inside who would help.

She turned toward the shadowed opening of the barn, imagining Radar's panic, confined in a horse trailer with fire exploding around him. When she found this cowardly kid, she intended to scare the shit out of him before sending him back to his grandmother's forgiving arms. "How is Radar doing now?" she asked.

"He's healing. Come see."

Nikki pulled in a fortifying breath. She was too much of an animal lover to be keen to see an injury, and dealing with Gunner's rehab had left her hyper sensitive to what four-legged partners risked every day on the job. But she steeled her shoulders and followed Lara inside the barn.

"There are seven police horses," Lara said, gesturing at the line of stalls. "Six officers, one spare horse. We do all the work ourselves. Feed, clean, groom plus manage our patrols. At the end of every ride, we go back and pick up manure from any streets with pedestrian traffic. That's so time consuming. Luckily the court often assigns someone to do that for community service. We've had everyone from shoplifters to sports and TV celebrities. Lately, Billy Tanner was working for us on the weekends...up until last Saturday."

"Was there anything different about that day?" Nikki asked. "Something that might have made him want to throw down his shovel?"

"Nothing that came from us," Lara said with a shrug. "He picked up manure around Main Street Mall. Checked the water troughs in a couple horse friendly alleys. There may have been some heckling, and a couple of the panhandlers can be a bit obnoxious. Nothing unusual though. Billy seemed cool with it all. And Smitty said everything was normal when the kid left for the night."

"So Smitty was the last one to see him?"

"Correct," Lara said, her voice a bit more crisp. "Smitty was the last officer here on Saturday."

The night Billy didn't return to his grandmother's house. "How did they get along?" Nikki asked. "It must have been a little tense. Especially for Smitty, considering it was his horse that Billy hurt."

"Maybe it was at first," Lara admitted. "But we all got over it. It was certainly convenient to have someone picking up our manure."

"Still, to have to see the teen who deliberately hurt Radar."

"I don't like where you're going with this," Lara said, aggressively hiking her gun belt. But she was petite and much shorter than Nikki's five foot six, so the move just looked amusing, like a kid dressed up as a cowboy struggling to handle a twenty-pound weight.

"Billy is one of the best workers we ever had," Lara added, her voice rising. "He saved us a lot of time and always volunteered to do more. Like I told you on the phone, we didn't run him off."

Nikki gave a soothing nod. Antagonizing this woman wouldn't help. Besides she didn't doubt Lara's facts; any friend of Justin's was trustworthy. But sometimes people formed the wrong impressions and it was Nikki's job to sift through it, no matter where it took her.

"We all liked Billy," Lara muttered, calming somewhat as she turned and continued down the aisle. "Maybe at first we got some digs in. Hazed him a bit. But media reports made Radar's injury sound like a deliberate murder attempt. And then that animal rights blogger exaggerated it even more. Billy always claimed he didn't know Radar was tied in the trailer, and after we got to know the kid, we believed him."

Nikki remained quiet. Most people liked to fill the silence and Lara was no exception. But Nikki made a mental note to dig up the blogger's post. Billy may not have a social media presence, but someone seemed to have thrust him into the limelight.

Lara stopped in front of an airy box stall surrounded by the smell of fresh shavings and the hint of aloe ointment. A tall black horse with a white face poked his head over the door, curious but untroubled.

"This is Radar," Lara said. The horse stretched his neck out until his head rested on Lara's shoulder. She affectionately scratched the underside of his jaw and he grunted, his eyes rolling in pleasure.

"The vet says he'll have scars," Lara said, "and the hair won't ever grow back around his spine. But he's going to be okay. Smitty is having a special saddle pad made. Radar might not be happy about walking onto a trailer again though so we'll have to work around that. Fortunately his lungs weren't damaged."

Nikki eyed the patchwork of black, pink and white skin. "It must have been horrible," she said, feeling another well of sympathy for this sweet horse. And another rush of anger at Billy.

"Yes. At first we wanted to throttle the kid. But honestly he seemed to feel bad. He certainly wasn't what we expected."

"How so?" Nikki said, still fighting her own ambivalence.

"He was polite, thoughtful," Lara said. "He often brought carrots for the horses. He lives east of the city and I think his grandmother has a vegetable garden. But how many fourteen-year-old boys would even think of hopping on a bus, lugging carrots for a horse? And he kept Radar's stall spotless. Always careful about infection."

Nikki rubbed her forehead. Maybe Mrs. Tanner hadn't been completely wrong with the glowing description of her grandson. But if so, that raised a more troubling question. Like what had really happened to Billy after he left the barn last Saturday?

Her mouth tightened in thought as her gaze swept beyond the aisle to a locked door. "Was there any theft that night?" she asked. "Did he have access to the tack? What else did Billy do here?"

"Anything we told him," Lara said, following Nikki's gaze. "He didn't just pick up manure. He cleaned tack, mixed feed, even groomed our horses. When he first came, he didn't know much but he quickly turned into a good stable hand. But he didn't have a tack room key, and he was always supervised."

"So nothing was missing? No drugs or anything?"

"No." Lara scowled and it was obvious her patience was running short. "And we don't keep drugs here. If we make a street bust, it's turned in immediately."

"What about equine drugs?"

"Well, naturally we have horse drugs here."

"And they're all accounted for?" Nikki knew for a fact that horse tranqs could put users in quite a stupor and were a cheap alternative to more expensive street drugs.

"Yes," Lara said. But her gaze flickered, and Nikki suspected the woman wasn't really certain.

"Billy didn't steal anything," Lara added. "We don't know why he left. But he saved us a lot of work so we all want him to come back and finish his hours."

"Even Smitty?"

"Especially Smitty. Looking after a burn victim is labor intensive. Radar's wounds require a lot of care, along with antibiotics and drugs for pain and itching. Billy worked weekends, nine to five, but he always stayed a few extra minutes to help Smitty."

"Is Smitty here now?" Nikki glanced around the barn, already knowing the answer to that question. The tack room was padlocked and Lara's truck was the only vehicle in the lot.

"Sorry, but you missed him." Lara's flippant tone showed she wasn't sorry at all. "Besides, Smitty doesn't know anything more than what I told you." Her voice hardened. "The police will find Billy. I suggest you forget this witch hunt and let his grandmother keep her money."

"And I suggest you give me Smitty's number," Nikki said. "So I can finish the job I was hired to do."

"Then leave a message at the office," Lara snapped. "Or if you have a business card, I'll give it to Smitty and ask him to call."

Nikki pulled out a card, wishing she'd arrived earlier. She wanted to question Smitty in person, preferably when he wasn't expecting her. But he was a cop. If he wanted to avoid her, he could. And would.

Lara took Nikki's business card, holding it at arm's length from her face, as if it might be tainted. "Nikki Drake Investigative Services," she sneered. "Licensed and bonded. Wow, a real PI. And here I thought you mainly tagged around after Justin."

The woman had been much nicer when she thought Justin and Nikki were only friends. And Nikki was tired of her attitude. She'd worked hard on controlling her temper but she'd never been one to ignore insults. And she wasn't in the mood to start now.

"No," she said. "I don't tag around after Justin. Mainly I sleep with him."

Lara's creamy complexion turned a mottled red. She turned on her heels, stomped to the tack room and unlocked the door. She stepped inside and stuck Nikki's card on an ancient fridge where it joined scores of business cards and takeout menus, held in place by an oversized Disney magnet.

She yanked open the fridge door and grabbed a bottle of water from beside a row of motley horse medications. Tilting her head, she guzzled half its contents. Clearly she was thirsty; it was hard to take breaks on a horse. And clearly this interview was over.

It had been helpful though. Lara's statement that Billy was a likeable kid and an excellent worker supported Mrs. Tanner's claim. Nikki hadn't expected to hear that. It changed her investigative process. She'd been planning to troll the streets, flashing his picture to some of her more reliable street contacts and asking them to put out the word that Billy should contact his family.

But the fact that Smitty had been the last person to see Billy—the officer whose innocent horse had been injured—was a red flag that couldn't be ignored. It also left her with a niggling sense of unease. She certainly didn't intend to wait until next week for Smitty to call. Understandably, the mounted police unit was a tight group and Lara wouldn't give out a co-worker's phone number. But there was always a way around road blocks. Maybe they shared a ritual Friday night drink and it would be possible to track Smitty down during his off hours.

"Thanks for your time," Nikki said to Lara's stiff back. "I appreciate it. Hopefully you can finish feeding the horses in time to join the others for a drink."

If Lara wouldn't reveal where their meeting spot was, Nikki thought, she'd simply follow the woman's silver truck. She hadn't been expecting to sit surveillance tonight, but fortunately she'd parked her Subaru out of sight. As far as she knew, Lara didn't know the make of her car. And the little compact was unobtrusive, perfect for staying unnoticed.

"I'm not joining the boys tonight. I have other plans." Lara twisted, tossing Nikki a cool smile. One that said she knew exactly what Nikki was planning. "But don't worry. I'll make sure Smitty calls you next week...if he has time."

Her words underscored that Smitty wouldn't be calling any time soon and Nikki stepped into the tack room, frustration clipping her words. "Hopefully he'll find the time," she said, "Because my client doesn't believe Billy ran away. If she's correct—and it's beginning to look as if she is—then Billy might need help. And a few more days could make a big difference. A critical difference."

"Don't play the guilt card," Lara said. "I'm not giving you Smitty's personal number. No way I'm stepping on his toes. I know you want to make a paying case out of this but you should leave him alone. Besides, the police are on top of it."

"But they haven't found him yet," Nikki said. "And we all want the same thing. I assumed Billy chose to leave too. But the more I hear, the more it seems possible it wasn't his choice to disappear."

Lara crossed her arms. "Smitty thinks he ran away," she muttered. "So do I."

"But we aren't certain. So until his grandmother knows he's safe, I plan to keep looking. Because he might have been abducted."

"Good God," Lara snapped. "Not every missing kid has been abducted. Don't be so stubborn. You don't know the police stats. I do. And you're affected way too much by what happened to your sister."

Low blow. Pain twisted inside Nikki's chest, accompanied by an angry flush that heated her entire body. But she wasn't going to be deterred by personal snipes. Persistence was an investigator's biggest asset. She intended to keep poking, even if she was dealing with a bunch of cops closing ranks. And the police stable was the logical starting point.

She pulled in a calming breath then forged on. "Smitty was the last known person to see Billy," she said. "Likely he had nothing to do with Billy's disappearance. But he might know something that could help. And I do know the stats. I also know what it feels like to have a family member go missing. Billy's grandmother is frantic. So I'm going to help—and I don't really care whose toes I step on."

"Well, I care," Lara said. "It's hard enough being low on the totem pole. Always getting the green horses. Smitty's my boss. He'll decide if he wants to call."

Now it was "if" not "when" he called. Nikki sighed. Clearly Lara wasn't going to pave the way to talking to a fellow cop but her resentment wasn't entirely work related. And Nikki wasn't above using that knowledge.

"Justin admires you," Nikki said. "Says you're a good cop. He thought you'd be able to help me, any way you can.

Lara groaned but lowered her arm, the water bottle still hanging from her hand. It was silent in the tack room, except for the ticking of the struggling fridge. Lara looked torn but Nikki didn't feel much sympathy. She was on Mrs. Tanner's side.

"You're wasting your time," Lara said, but with much less conviction. "It wasn't Smitty. He had nothing to do with it."

"Probably not. But I have to talk to him."

Lara pivoted and slammed the bottle into a nearby bin, splashing water over the side of the can. "Smitty's at the Rusty Nail," she muttered, her words escaping in a rush, as if fearing that they might not come out at all if she paused to reconsider. "He drives a black Ford pickup and lives outside the city. He has supper at the Nail and generally leaves around eight. If you hurry, you can catch him. Don't let him know I told you."

Nikki raised her hand in a grateful salute. "I won't," she said.

CHAPTER FIVE

Billy rolled onto his side, scraping the hay beneath him into a fluffier pile. A few stalks pricked through his shirt, yet it was surprisingly comfortable. There wasn't much hay, maybe a couple flakes, but it was sweet and fresh. A couple colder nights, he'd layered the hay over his chest for warmth. However, the naked prisoner in the adjacent stall had no hay whatsoever. It hurt to see the man constantly shivering.

"Hey, mister," Billy whispered, cautiously averting his head, hiding his mouth from the watchful eye of the surveillance camera. "You awake? It's a little warmer now."

He didn't expect an answer. The man barely moved and his groans had slowed over the last few days. Billy wasn't sure how long the man had been chained in the stall. He'd been there when Billy first woke, yet he always seemed too afraid to speak.

That first day, Billy had yelled and screamed and cursed. But the stun gun had quickly silenced him. He was terrified of the gun and how it made him piss his pants. Now low whispers were his only form of rebellion. It wasn't much, but it gave him some satisfaction that he was breaking the "no talking" rule. One tiny little thing still under his control. It didn't even matter that the man never answered. It was just comforting to have someone else in the barn.

"Don't give up, mister," Billy said. "I have forty-three kernels of corn. You can have them all."

He studied his piles of grain with a stab of wistfulness. He'd separated the mixture, assuming the corn and molasses would have the most food value. The tedious process gave him something to do these long hours when daylight filtered through the dusty window.

"But you have to eat them," Billy added. "Don't leave any on the floor where *he* can see and get mad."

"No use," came a faint voice.

"What? Did you say something?" Billy jerked to his feet so fast he stumbled over his jeans as they slid below his hips. He tugged them up with an impatient hand and hurried to the wall, desperate for companionship. "Want me to push the corn through?" Billy asked. "Then maybe we can figure a way to get out of here."

"No use," the man repeated, his voice eerily clear after not speaking for so long. "Tomorrow's Saturday...feeding day."

"But you can eat this now." Billy bent and scooped up the precious corn, cupping it in his hand. "And I'll give you more tomorrow when he feeds me."

The man remained curled in a ball. It was impossible to guess what he needed most: food or water. Billy had stopped shitting days ago but he still peed regularly in the far corner, as far away from his hay bed as his chain allowed.

This man's stall though was bare and dry, devoid of food or human waste.

Billy dropped the corn and scooped a handful of water from his bucket, flicking it through the steel mesh and into the adjacent stall. Drops scattered on the wood around the man's lank hair but a few hit his neck. One even pooled in the middle of his back, where his spine protruded in rounded knobs.

The man jerked as if shocked. He rolled over, staring up at Billy, his expression turning from fear to resignation. His cheek bones were the most prominent part of his face, his eyes sunken. Earlier Billy had pegged the guy as being in his thirties. Now his dull skin was so cracked, he looked older than Billy's grandmother.

"My dog died like this," the man said. "Only God can help me now." Ignoring the droplets of precious water, he curled back into a tight ball.

"Don't give up, mister," Billy said. "Please. Lick up the water. Then I'll throw some food."

But the man had retreated back into his silent shell, his curled form reeking of hopelessness. And Billy sank to the floor beside the scatter of yellow corn, confused, afraid and very much alone.

CHAPTER SIX

Nikki whipped her Subaru into the last remaining spot of the Rusty Nail's cramped parking lot. She preferred to back into spaces. One never knew when it would be necessary to leave quickly. But it was almost eight o'clock, and according to Lara, Smitty didn't usually stay past that hour.

She scanned the parking area, hoping that he was still here. Several pickups were jammed in the lot, including two Fords. The one closest to her car had some hay bales stacked in the back. The truck was too dusty to tell if it was black or blue. But the parking decal on the windshield matched the one on Sgt. Lara McCullough's silver truck.

Satisfied, Nikki slid from the car and strode toward the entrance, phone in her hand as she pulled up the publicity page of the Mounted Police Unit. Lots of horse pictures, a few of Lara, and finally she found Sgt. Aaron Smith, aka Smitty.

She paused on the walkway, taking the time to enlarge Smitty's image, hoping it was a recent photo. Smile lines around blue eyes, straight nose, stubborn jaw. Not a bad-looking guy. The accompanying blurb stated he'd been a member of the police force for twelve years and was an active volunteer with the local 4-H Club. He also helped maintain the county fairgrounds, organize youth shows and assisted in horse rescue.

That last tidbit was revealing. Obviously Smitty was an avid horse lover, not the type who would view Radar as simply a tool for policing. And every day Smitty had to go to work where he was reminded of how Billy had hurt his horse. It must have been frustrating, despite what Lara had said. Had Smitty lost his temper last Saturday? Maybe smacked the kid a little too hard?

Nikki shoved her phone back in her pocket and hurried to the entrance of the Rusty Nail. The wooden door swung open, almost hitting her. She stepped sideways. Two men spilled out, their voices jovial, thick with the smell of beer and testosterone.

"Come on in, beautiful," the first man said, theatrically pulling the door back.

"I see the clientele here just improved," the second man said. "One hundred percent."

"It's mostly cops in there now," the first man added. "That's why we're headed for the Midtown. But we could stay for another drink. Keep those stiffs away from you."

"Thanks," Nikki said with a grin. "But I'm meeting one of them."

They guffawed, still filling the doorway. She brushed past, feeling their leers but unbothered by them. Much of her work involved solitary work in bars much seedier than this one.

Once inside, she cut to the right, moving as if she knew where she was going, barely turning her head as she checked out the clientele, mostly men dressed in sweats or jeans with a couple wearing off-the-rack suits. Probably lawyers, she decided, hoping to find some loose tongues. The Rusty Nail was a real guys' bar, the type of place where one could enjoy a drink, play pool or pick up company for the night. A few years ago it had been frequented by sports fans. Now it appeared to be a magnet for law enforcement.

It took a moment to spot Smitty, seated at a square table with two other men. One of his tablemates had such a baby face, she wondered if the guy was even legal. Their plates were pushed to the side, topped with a scatter of fries, ketchup smears and balled-up napkins. Good, they were finished eating. She'd learned not to get in the way of a man and his appetite.

"Hello," she said, pausing by Smitty's chair. "My name is Nikki. Could I speak with you for a moment? Perhaps by the bar?"

Smitty's head jerked up, his eyes widening. "Certainly, darling," he said, scooping up his beer. He scraped back his chair, shot his buddies a triumphant grin and sauntered to the bar.

"What would you like to drink?" he asked, pulling out her stool and signaling the bartender.

"Not a thing, thank you." She flicked open her credentials and passed him a business card. "I'm a private investigator and just want to ask some questions about Billy Tanner."

Smitty's smile faded, replaced with a scowl. "Fine," he said. "But what's your stake in this? You think the police can't handle it?"

"They're treating Billy as a runaway. His grandmother isn't so sure. I just need your impression of his state of mind when he left your barn last Saturday."

"His state of mind was okay. Like always," Smitty said, waving away the bartender. "He's a very level kid."

"Billy picked up manure in front of the mall that afternoon," Nikki said. "Was there much interaction with other teens? Anything different?"

"He was always hassled a bit," Smitty said. "Sometimes I felt sorry for him. But dammit, he deserved it. Did you see what he did to my horse?"

"I did. And I'm sorry. It must have been difficult."

Smitty's face hardened. He clenched his fist, absently tracing his fingers over the knuckles of his right hand. Judging from the pink skin, the fire hadn't left him unscathed. "I got Radar out of the trailer that night. He was so brave. I wanted to chase down all those punks but my horse needed me."

"Why was only Billy charged?"

"He was the only one visible on our camera. He was quick to confess but claimed he didn't know any of the others. Besides, he was the one who threw the bottle. If he had any priors, we would have crucified him."

"His grandmother feels he *was* crucified by the media," Nikki said. "She showed me the clippings."

There had been considerable press when the police horse had been fire bombed and the news had remained frontline for more than a week. Animal activist groups had jumped on the story, with reactions ranging from heartfelt sympathy to blatant hostility. One extremist group in the UK even suggested Billy be burned too, so that he'd understand the pain he inflicted. And Nikki hadn't yet seen the blog Lara had mentioned.

That was another troubling thing about this case. Despite that Billy was a minor, somehow his name had leaked. But he hadn't disappeared at the height of the turmoil. As Mrs. Tanner had pointed out, it was odd he would run away now, after the furor had subsided.

Smitty raised the palms of his hands. "Not my fault that details got out. People can find anything if they dig deep and are a little savvy."

"Yes, some organizations are surprisingly savvy," she said. "With a nudge in the desired direction."

"If you're insinuating I leaked his name to the animal rights people, try and prove it."

"I'm not interested in proving it," Nikki said. "I just want to find Billy. It would help if I knew what triggered him on Saturday."

"Well, it wasn't the press or any stupid blog." Smitty's shoulders relaxed slightly. "The story was cold. And Saturday Billy seemed normal. He stayed late, picking off some dead skin from Radar's back. He had nice hands, a gentle touch."

Had. Smitty spoke about Billy in the past tense but this wasn't the time to push. Already the man was glancing over his shoulder, close to walking away.

"Did you see Billy talking to anyone by the mall?" she asked, keeping her voice companionably soft. "Anything notable?"

"He was teased a bit when he was picking up manure but only the usual heckling. And that kid was tough. I didn't want to like him, but I did."

That matched with Lara's comment and Nikki gave an agreeable nod. "So everything was routine up to the point when he left to catch the bus?"

"That's right," Smitty said.

But his eyes flickered, shifting to the left. Something about the bus?

"His grandmother said the bus stop was only a stone's throw from their house," Nikki went on, watching Smitty's expression.

"Generally runaways don't go home." His mouth curved in a faint sneer. "That's why they're called runaways."

She took a calming breath. "But we don't know if he deserves that label."

"Sure he does. I spotted him a few days ago but he bolted when I hollered."

"Where was that?"

"Near Main Street Mall, just past the Cannabis Club."

"Are you sure it was him?"

"Yes," Smitty snapped. "Obviously he got tired of working for us."

"You're probably right," Nikki said, making an agreeable sound even though she wasn't buying it. "Did bus surveillance pick up anything?"

"We already checked that. He didn't get on his bus which proves he stayed in town." Smitty raised his beer in an ironic gesture. "Look, it's great you digging but it's best to let the police handle it. With our resources, we'll find him much quicker than you."

"It's been a week."

"Yes," Smitty said. "And it might take us another couple weeks."

"But what if Billy is hurt somewhere?"

Smitty gave a dismissive grunt and rose from his stool. "I've come to learn that these kids are all the same. He'll show up in his own time. No doubt he's tired of working his ass off."

"But this is out of character," Nikki said, swiveling around on her stool so she could face Smitty. She didn't like how he towered over her, but she didn't want to stand up and show her discomfort. "His grandmother says he's never disappeared before. Barely missed a day of school. And anytime he stayed out late, he called."

Smitty snorted. "Despite his grandmother's high opinion, that kid isn't lily white."

"But this was his first offence. So he *was* lily white until the fire. Why did it even happen? Why did he target your barn?"

Smitty dragged a hand over his jaw as if he'd never considered the reason.

"His brother, Jack, had been in trouble before," Nikki went on. "But not Billy. Were you Jack's arresting officer? Or any of your other mounted officers?"

"You're way off base," Smitty muttered, folding his arms and shifting back a step. "We had no history with Jack. We never even knew about his little street gang. And how does this help find Billy?"

"Just trying to figure out his motivation. Maybe Billy was trying to get back at the police because of something that happened to his brother. Every bit of information helps."

"There was nothing like that," Smitty said. "And I don't have time for any more of this shit. You need to leave now. Next time, call the station first."

He stomped back toward his cop friends, so determined to escape her questions that he forgot his beer.

Nikki sighed. Of course she was going to leave the Rusty Nail but not because Smitty had given her walking orders. Out of pure stubbornness she remained seated on her stool, waiting for him to come back and collect his drink. Besides, something felt wrong. So far Smitty had been the first person to quiver her radar. He seemed genuine about liking Billy but he was holding something back.

There'd definitely been some evasiveness about the bus.

She waited until the bartender moved out of earshot, then called Billy's grandmother. "Do you know what time the last bus left the city, assuming Billy was late and missed his regular ride?"

"The last bus is 8:15," Mrs. Tanner said. "But Billy didn't ever take that one. It involved a transfer and a mile walk in the dark. Even though there's hardly any traffic on our road, some idiots move at a good clip, especially when they're lost. Oh, no!" Her voice changed from disdain of lost drivers to sheer horror. "Do you think he's hurt? That he's lying in a ditch somewhere?"

"No," Nikki said quickly. "I only want to check some more bus cameras. The police didn't spot him on his regular bus. But maybe he found some friends and stayed downtown for a few hours."

"Billy wouldn't do that. He always came home on time."

Nikki gave a reluctant smile. The woman was definitely stubborn in her beliefs. "Did he ever mention hanging out around Main Street Mall?" she asked.

"Absolutely not. The prices are outrageous there. And with schoolwork, chores and community service, he was way too busy." Her voice rose. "You're wasting valuable time. And you're not listening to what I already told you."

Nikki pushed on. "Actually someone thought they saw him hanging out at the mall a few days ago."

"Then they're lying."

Maybe. Nikki glanced across the room at Smitty. He didn't seem inclined to come back and get his beer, a pricey non-alcoholic one that he'd barely touched. In fact, he'd just signaled the waiter for a fresh drink. Smitty's gaze met hers and she gave him a cheery wave. He scowled, shifting his chair so that she could only see his rigid back.

"Will you call me tonight?" Mrs. Tanner asked. "If you see Billy on a bus video? That would prove he's not downtown, right?"

"The offices are closed now," Nikki said. "But we'll talk tomorrow. I'd like to come out to your house and have a look around."

"Should I send Jack out to check the ditches?"

"No, Mrs. Tanner," Nikki said. "We really don't think Billy was on any of the later buses. It's just something I want to rule out."

"Billy always left the police barn between 5:00 and 5:15. And he never stayed late in town." Mrs. Tanner's voice choked. "But at least you're asking questions. And looking."

"I'll be out around one o'clock tomorrow," Nikki said gently. "Try to get some sleep." She waited for Mrs. Tanner to cut the connection then slid off the stool.

Scooping up Smitty's deserted drink, she strode to his table and set the bottle down in front of him.

"See you later, Smitty," she said, ignoring his slit-eyed stare and the puzzled glances of his tablemates.

She stepped outside, relieved to breathe fresh air again. The night was cool, heavy with fog. The only light over the parking lot was burned out, leaving the vehicles shrouded in darkness. She scanned both sides of the lot, holding her keys in her right hand, the long vehicle key exposed and pointed like a weapon.

The parking area had emptied and gaps flanked her car. She appreciated that, was more comfortable being able to see her surroundings in that vulnerable moment when one focused on opening the door.

She passed behind Smitty's dusty pickup. Unlike Lara's shiny truck, this vehicle looked like it had covered some hard miles. The deep-treaded tires and rugged trailer hitch indicated it was a bona fide work vehicle. Perhaps he pulled the police trailer with this pickup. He'd been first on the scene, the officer who had rushed into the trailer and rescued Radar. But since Smitty lived outside the city and was an active volunteer, he obviously used the truck for other purposes. A vehicle could tell a lot about its owner—especially the interior.

She checked over her shoulder. The door to the bar remained closed, the entrance deserted. Besides, it was doubtless anyone would see her in the dark.

She stepped onto the back bumper and peered into the truck bed. Spotted four hay bales, a heavy tow chain, and countless squashed paper cups. Clearly Smitty regularly chucked his empty cups into the back.

Placing her hands over the top of the tailgate, she vaulted lightly onto the back. She scooped up several cups and gave them an experimental sniff. Only coffee. Some cops were closet drinkers but it appeared Smitty didn't indulge. He even drank non-alcoholic beer on Friday night.

She tossed the cups aside and turned to leave. But something sticky clung to her foot. She pulled out her phone and ran the light around her feet. A dark stain covered at least eight inches of the truck floor, partially hidden by the hay bales.

Wetting the tip of her finger, she bent and rubbed at the smear. She pulled her hand away and inspected her finger. Stared a long moment, filled with conflicting emotion. Because the red on her finger was unmistakably blood.

The bar door opened, spilling light into the parking lot. She dropped behind the tailgate, her heart pounding. But it wasn't Smitty, just one of the guys who'd been sitting at his table, the young one with the round face. He whistled in the dark as he ambled to his vehicle.

His car was parked close to Smitty's, much too close for comfort, and she flattened herself closer to the truck bed, grateful the guy wasn't driving a pickup. He would have spotted her in an instant. She waited until his vehicle crunched from the lot, using the time to steady her breathing. And her suspicions.

The blood probably wasn't Billy's. There were plenty of reasons why Smitty might have blood in the back of his truck. But right now she couldn't think of a single one.

She scooted up to the sliding rear window and peered inside. The cab appeared spotless, well-kept. There was no blinking alarm, only a benign GPS mounted on the dash. She jiggled the window, guessing that even if it had been left unlocked, it would be a tight squeeze. And an illegal search.

The back window slid open, surprising her. She quit worrying about getting stuck or the legalities and slid through the opening, landing awkwardly on the bench seat.

She straightened and switched on the GPS, her fingers clumsy with urgency. It seemed agonizingly slow and she checked over the dashboard, her gaze shooting between the door of the bar and the lit screen.

Smitty's driving history finally appeared. At first glance his routes seemed typical. A couple airport trips as well as forays north to San Francisco—it looked like he was a 49ers fan—but mostly commutes between his home in the southeast and the police barn. Yet as she dug deeper, an unusual number of secondary roads were displayed. She'd have to check some of the coordinates but it definitely put him within twenty miles of Billy's home. It didn't prove much though, just that he liked to drive around the countryside.

The bar door swung open. Light sliced the night and Smitty's big shoulders were silhouetted in the doorway.

She dropped to the floor, her throat drying in panic. He was too close. He'd see her if she crawled out the back window.

She wiggled over the floor of the cab toward the passenger's seat, drew in a fortifying breath, then cautiously clicked open the door. The interior light came on and an alarm blared next to her ears, shattering the stillness.

She slid to the ground, grateful that the piercing alarm muffled her footsteps.

"Hey, stop!" she called even as she bolted into the darkness.

She sprinted about twenty feet, pretending to chase an intruder before turning in mock resignation. She didn't have to pretend to be breathing hard. Her chest was knotted with adrenaline, and admittedly, fear.

"What the hell?" Smitty bellowed. He hurried around the back of his truck and reached into his pocket.

"It was kids, trying to break in." Nikki gestured over her shoulder. "They ran when I saw them. I don't think they took anything."

Smitty found his remote, pointed it at the pickup and the blaring alarm stopped. He swung open the cab door and scanned the interior.

"Looks like they crawled in through the back window," Nikki said helpfully.

"Tight squeeze," Smitty said, sliding the window shut. He turned, his face shadowed. "What are you still doing here?"

"I'm going downtown to check for Billy in some soup kitchens. I was just sitting in my car, gathering addresses."

"Gathering addresses?" He stepped closer. The guy seemed even bigger in the dark. "Did you want to see something from my truck? Maybe my GPS?"

She couldn't make out his expression but he sounded almost amused, as if he was playing with her. As if he knew she'd been the one to squeeze through that window.

"Not necessary. I have one on my cell. I was just looking at it. See?" She waved her phone and stepped back but nervousness kept her talking. "Guess I'll leave now and check the usual spots, you know, where *runaways* go."

"You do that," Smitty said, and now his voice was totally flat. "But you need to be more careful. Next time there might not be any police around to help. A little lady like you, working alone, could get hurt."

She gave him a look, pretending she didn't know what he was talking about and turned away. But it was obvious he knew she'd been snooping. She could feel his hard gaze boring into her back as she walked toward her car.

Her breathing didn't settle until she slid behind the wheel. And heard the comforting click of her door lock.

CHAPTER SEVEN

Nikki pressed her remote, waiting as the garage door at Justin's house smoothly opened. She backed into one of the two parking slots and entered the house through the side door. It was quicker to park outside but Justin was a stickler for security. As a high-profile detective, he'd made a lot of enemies. Her career as an investigator wasn't nearly as illustrious. Gunner was helping though. His keen nose had found her sister and his intimidating presence was proving to be invaluable. Not to mention, he was her best friend. Along with Justin.

She kicked off her shoes, poured herself a glass of wine and pressed Justin's number. He answered on the second ring.

"Something came up," she said. "And it's too late to drive back to the K9 center. So I'm at your place tonight."

He was silent for a moment. Then: "I'll be home in forty minutes. Order something from Vinny's."

"Delivery or do you want to pick it up?"

"Delivery. I don't want to waste any time." His chuckle was low and sexy, and made her heart kick.

Admittedly finding time to spend together was challenging. When Justin was working a fresh case, he was rarely home so she'd been sleeping most nights at the center, two hours away. She wanted to ask if he'd made any inroads on his current case, but he'd already cut the connection, a sure sign he was immersed in his work. However, she had no doubt that he'd be home within the hour. Justin was always reliable.

She checked his fridge—milk, eggs but little else—then called Vinny's and placed a huge order. That way Justin would have leftovers available for a few days.

"I'll have your food there quickly," Vinny promised, pausing to deliver rapid-fire directions to the kitchen staff. "How's the patient?" he asked, returning to the phone and switching from Italian back to English.

"Improving. He started water therapy today."

"When Gunner comes home," Vinny said, "I'll make him a special treat. It's strange not to see the two of you together. But don't worry. I had a friend with a three-legged dog and he did just fine. Everything will work out."

Nikki made an agreeable sound but steered the topic to menu prices and the rising cost of Italian flour, Vinny's pet peeve lately, and a topic that was guaranteed to distract him. He went on to talk about his take-out service and how he'd started joint advertising with a new restaurant that served real Halifax donairs.

It seemed she'd barely hung up when the doorbell chimed, announcing a delivery. The surveillance feed showed the guy's arms were loaded with brown paper bags. Vinny had clearly doubled her order. If Justin didn't want it in his fridge, she'd take it back to the center. The technicians and trainers were always grateful when she left food in the staff room.

The driver passed over the food, thanking her profusely for the size of her tip before bouncing back to his car. She closed the door and reset the alarm. Had barely placed the boxes on the counter when the garage door rumbled open.

Moments later, Justin strolled through the attached door.

He gave her a too-short kiss then lifted his head and gave an appreciative sniff. "Are we expecting company?" he asked, his arm looped around her waist even as he eyed the amount of food with suspicion.

"No, as usual Vinny is just very generous."

Justin's mouth curved in a relieved smile. He flicked an experimental finger over one of the boxes. "And as usual, it was a speedy delivery. In fact, it feels a bit too hot to eat. Perhaps we should let it cool?"

Her face was still tilted, ready to welcome another kiss, but she managed a composed smile. "Of course," she said. "What should we do while we wait? Maybe burn a few calories in your gym?"

"I'd prefer we burn them elsewhere," he said.

"Like in your bedroom?" Her words came out rather sultry for a supposedly tough PI. But Justin had that effect on her. And on other women as well.

"What an excellent idea." He scooped her up, his mouth so close to her cheek she could feel his teasing grin. "Glad you thought of it."

Nikki gave a luxurious stretch then snuggled into Justin's shoulder. His bedroom was definitely more enjoyable than his gym. He had such a wide range of workout equipment she still hadn't tried everything. But she intended to work up a sweat after he left. Jogging around the K9 field helped with her aerobic exercise. But she wanted to target some core muscles, maybe work with his weights. No doubt she'd be doing a lot of lifting when Gunner came home.

She felt Justin's scrutiny and tilted her head, staring into his enigmatic eyes. "How's he doing?" Justin asked, as if reading her mind.

"Still improving," she said. "I guess it's just a wait and see."

"Do you have everything you need? Tony said you've been helping on the obstacle field in between monitoring Gunner's rehab. But that you weren't there today?"

Nikki fought a stab of irritation. Tony Lambert managed the K9 center and seemingly reported her every move to Justin. She knew her annoyance revealed a double standard since she gratefully accepted Justin's influence whenever it could help Gunner. And she was one of the few civilians to ever be offered a dorm room at the center.

"I wasn't there," Nikki said, "because Sonja called me about a possible client."

"That's good. You need more to do than build dog ramps and worry about Gunner." Justin's empathy made her feel guilty for her prickliness. "Did you take the case?"

"I did," she said. "In fact I already questioned Lara about it."

"How's Lara?" he asked, and if there was anything more than polite interest in his voice, Nikki didn't hear it. In fact, he was already turning to check the time, and she guessed he'd be racing out in minutes, likely eating his food in the car.

"She's fine. And her horse, Guinness, the one we saw being schooled a while back is fine as well."

"I'm glad he's working out. He's quite a switch from her previous mount."

"How so?" Nikki asked, knowing Justin could talk horses for hours and if any subject could keep him relaxed and in bed, it would be that. He never looked tired but she didn't know how he could function with so little sleep.

Justin rolled toward her, idly running his hand in circles on her back and she closed her eyes in pleasure. He had the best hands, whether it was handling criminals, horses. Or her.

"Could you scratch a little higher," she said with a sigh. "While we talk about the next time we go to the horse races, and, you know, who we should bet for the Pacific Classic?"

Justin chuckled. "The Classic isn't until August. But I'm not going back to the office until morning. Do you want to talk about your new case?"

"I just want you to get some food and sleep," she said, tilting her head and planting a kiss on his chest. "And my work is very boring compared to your murder cases, especially that unfortunate judge."

Justin didn't talk much about his work, preferring to put it aside when they were together. When he did speak though, she always learned a lot. She didn't want to probe, but it was public knowledge that Judge Kirby's ears had been hacked off and then delivered to a horrified journalist. When the judge had first disappeared, it had been front page news then slowly faded, despite the family's offer of a substantial reward. Now the gruesome ear delivery had boosted his abduction back into the spotlight, driving home the fact that police still had no real suspects.

"Are you sure the judge is even dead?" she asked.

"Most assuredly," Justin said dryly. "The ears had significant bone and tissue attached."

Nikki suppressed her wince. *That* hadn't been revealed to the public. Although the fact that he'd had numerous affairs had been heavily publicized. "His poor family," she murmured, feeling an ache in her throat.

"They had no children," Justin said, "so his wife is dealing with it alone. It's been hell on her. She already closed their kennel. Sold every dog right down to the last Doberman puppy."

"Maybe one of the pups will end up in police training."

"Doubtful. The judge concentrated on the show ring. Bred dogs for over thirty years and was a judge for almost as long. Some of the performance qualities were watered down."

That made sense. Gunner had come from a long line of dogs bred for military and police work and even he had failed to pass the rigorous training. Although an abusive handler hadn't helped. Yet it had worked out beautifully for her since Justin had given her Gunner. She'd never had a better partner.

"I gather you're looking for that teen who skipped out on his service," Justin said, surprising her with his awareness. He seemed to have the scoop on everything, at all police levels. Still, this was quick. Even for him.

"How did you know?" she asked. "Was it because I visited Lara?"

"Partly. And also because you wouldn't have taken the case unless it was important. Running down insurance scammers or vetting employees would never have pulled you away from Gunner."

She gave a reluctant nod. Justin knew her well, probably better than she knew herself. Sometimes that bothered her. But he was the one who had brought up the case, giving her the chance to run some things by him.

"Do you know Sgt. Aaron Smith?" she asked. "Mounted unit. Works with Lara."

"No, but I remember when he was moved in to head that group. It's a tight bunch, popular in the community. Damn shame when one of their horses was burned. Lara mentioned that the kid had skipped out."

"Allegedly," Nikki said. "I've been hired to find out if he really did run." And then she absorbed what else Justin had said. Had he seen Lara this week?

"Your investigation won't be popular with the police," Justin went on. "Hurting one of their horses is like attacking a K9. You know how that feels."

"I do," she said, trying to straighten her thoughts. She'd never been the jealous type and she wasn't going to start questioning Justin about his friends or activities. Not unless it could help her with a case. Of course, Lara was related to Billy's case...

"I actually used your name with Lara today," she said, deliberately shifting her hand to the left side of Justin's chest. "I may have implied that you wanted her to help me."

"Good. Use whatever means you have to gather information. But you should know I'm not Lara's favorite person right now." He gave a rueful chuckle. "When I called asking about a breeder who knew the judge, she was rather cool."

Beneath Nikki's hand, Justin's heartbeat remained slow and steady. Reassuringly so. Whatever was going on with Lara seemed to be one way.

"You think another breeder killed him?" Nikki asked, relaxing against his shoulder.

"No, I'm just hoping for a break. It's been months and we've got nothing. No motive. No body. Only the ears."

That wouldn't be good for his solve rate. Although stats and accolades didn't drive Justin. He wanted to fight crime, to help people. He'd been like that since he was a teen. He was the best person she knew.

"I told his wife we'd find the killer," Justin said. "But it's looking grim. We're short staffed and the lab is still backlogged."

Nikki sighed. Justin was the type who followed through on a promise but unfortunately the city's murder rate hadn't slowed.

"Can I help?" she asked. "Want me to gather info on the breeder?"

"We've already done that. So far he's not a suspect, just another disgruntled competitor ready to throw more muck. He's gathered a bunch of material over the years that he claims proves tainted show results. We already know Kirby wasn't the most ethical of judges...or men."

"Hard to believe someone would kill just because their dog didn't win a blue ribbon."

"It's a long shot. Probably nothing in the material will help. But we'll comb through it. We all know how crazy people can be about their dogs." Justin's voice lowered a notch. "Like how you deserted me... And moved to the center."

Nikki gave him a teasing jab. It was doubtful he felt it though since his arm was so hard it hurt her hand. But she hadn't deserted him. Justin barely came home except to sleep. Admittedly though, her thoughts had been focused on Gunner.

"Would it help if I picked up the boxes for you?" she asked.

"Definitely. But the breeder lives thirty miles east of the city. Opposite direction to the K9 center."

"No problem. My client lives out that way too." It would help keep Mrs. Tanner's bill low if Nikki could split mileage with another account. The feisty woman would love the fact that the police were covering part of her bill.

"Thank you, Nik." Justin yawned and closed his eyes, as if taking one small thing off his plate had lightened his load enough to sleep. Clearly he wasn't in any hurry to go downstairs and eat.

She knew he'd recharge quickly; he was the master of catnaps. But she couldn't keep her mind off the waiting food. The protein bar she'd eaten during the drive back seemed like ages ago, and mouth-watering odors were wafting up the stairs. Garlic, tomato, onion. It had been weeks since she'd enjoyed Vinny's excellent cooking and her gut kicked with impatience. Yet she lay unmoving, giving Justin a chance to fall asleep, and just hoping her rumbling stomach didn't jar him awake.

"Go ahead and eat," Justin said with a chuckle, proving that his eyes might be shut but he was still catlike in his alertness. "And take some pictures tomorrow as well. Dogs, kennel, anything that might give us insight into how this guy is thinking. Doubt you'll see much of interest but at least then you can bill us for a full day...Lara mentioned that the Tanner family is struggling."

Gratitude warmed her chest. Justin appeared tough, but he was compassionate to the core, especially to the disadvantaged. And Nikki hadn't been the one to reveal the Tanners' financial challenges. Surprisingly it had been Lara.

"I didn't think Lara was worried about Billy or his grandmother," Nikki said, brushing a heartfelt kiss over Justin's cheek before easing from the bed.

"She's torn," Justin said, his voice drowsy. "Until Smitty insisted on a switch, Radar was her mount."

Nikki stilled, her legs draped over the side of the bed. She'd been focused on Smitty, solely because Radar was his horse. But Radar had been Lara's partner too. She remembered the way Radar had laid his big head on Lara's shoulder, his trust apparent. But Lara hadn't mentioned that. Had it been intentional or had it simply not come up?

She pulled in a pensive breath, glad Justin couldn't see her expression. "Good to know," she said.

CHAPTER EIGHT

The pigs were restless this morning. Billy didn't know why he hated them so much, only that their squeals always made him shiver. The sounds of their greedy rooting had been the first thing he'd heard when he woke to find himself imprisoned.

Obviously the man chained in the hell hole beside him felt the same way. The man was whispering about pigs, senseless incomprehensible words, but at least he was talking. Billy rose, starved for companionship—then stilled.

The back door clicked open, letting in a flood of daylight.

Billy sank back to his knees, hunched with fear, wishing he could turn invisible. Even without the stun gun and syringes, his tall captor was terrifying.

But the man ignored him. He walked to the adjacent stall, his stride long and purposeful. Slid open the heavy wooden door and stepped inside.

"Do you understand your transgressions?" the man asked. "That justice must be served before release?"

He spoke softly, like a normal person, and Billy's head lifted, buoyed with hope. It sounded like they were going to be released.

"Pl-please," the starving man whimpered. "I'm sorry."

"You were morally obligated to look after your dog. But you failed him."

"I was busy. I forgot. Please—"

"Animals have rights too. And atrocities committed against them cannot be tolerated." The man's voice rose. "Violence and neglect will be turned back to the perpetrator. Only then can all species live in harmony."

Billy clenched his hands together. The man sounded smart, almost like the lawyer his grandmother had hired back when Jack had that court trouble. Maybe he should speak up, plead his case. He liked animals, and always took Sparky on walks and fed him on time. He shouldn't be here. This was all a mistake.

Were the police pulling another gag on him, laughing when he pissed his pants? But even they wouldn't go to this much trouble. And the man in the stall wasn't pretending; he was truly starving. If Billy's mouth wasn't so bone dry—if he wasn't so utterly terrified of drawing their captor's attention—he'd ask some questions.

"I'm sorry," the man whispered, so low and weak Billy could barely hear. "I should have checked his bowl."

"So you repent?"

"Yes, yes, I do." The man was whimpering now, his fear contagious. "But please, don't do this. Please don't kill me—"

Billy wrapped his arms around his legs, too terrified to leave his safe corner and peer through the crack. His teeth clamped together so tightly he tasted blood. But he heard everything: the gasps, a bump, one last grunt. Then the sharp smell of urine, all horrifying details that his brain didn't want to process. He stuffed a hand over his mouth, blocking his whimpers. This was all horribly real.

The shuffling noise stopped. A wheelbarrow rolled down the aisle. Minutes later a meat saw hummed, and the air in the barn thickened with the smell of blood and bones. The pigs' grunts turned to squeals of anticipation.

And then Billy understood. Bile climbed his throat. And he couldn't stop gagging.

CHAPTER NINE

"Can you repeat that?" Nikki asked, her hand gripping the phone as she listened to her source within the police department. The man who'd trained Nikki had stressed that developing contacts was eighty percent of an investigator's job. And Ava Simmons was an excellent source, a clerk in the department with a very active social life. Ava had been open to swapping business favors and regularly asked Nikki to check out her dating partners, both male and female.

"Yes," Ava said. "I checked the routes you requested and can confirm a teenager who looked like Billy Tanner boarded the bus at 8:17 pm. He disembarked at 9:24 at the last stop, way out in the sticks."

Nikki stiffened. That meant the police were looking for Billy in the wrong place. He wasn't hanging out in any back alley. He'd actually left the city, just much later than anyone expected. And this was the route Mrs. Tanner had said Billy didn't take, the one that stopped a long mile from his house.

"Was he alone?" Nikki asked.

"As far as I can tell."

One good thing anyway, Nikki thought. "So the police search will be widened?"

"Probably," Ava said. "Once county is notified. But I assumed you'd want the chance to collar him first. Robert used to get real hot if his investigative work was wasted and the police took the credit."

Nikki's mouth tightened. She didn't like to be compared to her retired mentor. Preferred to bury his memory. And she just wanted Billy safely located; it didn't matter who found him. Of course, it helped that money wasn't important. A recent insurance payout meant she didn't have to worry about a pay check now, not as much as many other investigators.

"Thanks, Ava," Nikki said. "But the quicker Billy is found the better." She scanned her office notes, checking for the name of Ava's latest lover. "How's it going with Erin?" she asked.

"Our relationship is over. I'm going to run solo for a bit."

That would last for about a week, Nikki thought. Ava was constantly in and out of love. "Okay, well I owe you one," Nikki said. "Thanks for being so quick."

She cut the connection, her mind weighing all the possibilities. Last night, Smitty's GPS showed he hadn't been within ten miles of the Tanner's house. And the fact that Billy boarded a bus seemed to exonerate the man. But Mrs. Tanner claimed Billy always took the early bus. What had he done in those missing hours?

And though that last stop was far from the area shown on Smitty's GPS, it was still in the eastern county. Close enough to warrant more questions. Smitty would not be happy to see her again. Neither would Lara. But Lara hadn't been open about the fact that Radar used to be her horse. And Smitty couldn't be dismissed either.

Nikki shoved back her chair, her gaze shooting to Gunner's empty bed. This would have been a fun day for him. He loved horses and car rides in the country. Visiting the police barn and Mrs. Tanner's house would have ticked all his boxes. Plus there would be the visit to the Doberman breeder. The crux of the matter was that she missed her dog. She'd only had him for two years. Now she felt vulnerable without him.

She unlocked her gun drawer and placed the Glock in her backpack. She didn't always carry a weapon, content to rely on her martial arts training and, of course, Gunner. But she didn't have him beside her now, and she had the nagging sense that Billy was in trouble. Of course, the kid might be camping in the woods behind his house, sneaking into his grandmother's kitchen and helping himself to peanut butter sandwiches, bummed about his lengthy community service.

Deep down though, she didn't believe he was camping. And she had a psychic friend who might be able to confirm if her fears were justified. Better still, Sonja might be able to help find Billy.

Nikki rushed down the hall to the adjacent office: Sonja's Psychic and Parties. She and Sonja had a coffee date later this morning but Nikki's day was heating up. She'd have to cancel. Change it to dinner. Or maybe Sonja would want to come over and help clean up last night's leftovers.

Nikki jerked to a stop, slumping in disappointment when she saw Sonja's closed door. Lights glowed from behind the tinted window but the "In Session" door tag was draped over the handle. It would be rude to disturb her when she had a client, something Nikki was always careful not to do.

She tapped out a hasty text, cancelling their get-together and asking Sonja to call. Then she jogged to the back alley to collect her car, propelled by a sense of growing urgency.

Twenty minutes later, Nikki eased her Subaru to the curb behind the police barn. She cut her ignition, eyeing the parking lot. Three vehicles were parked beyond the steel mesh. The morning sun shimmered over Lara's silver truck but Smitty's pickup was absent. No horses were turned out in the paddock so it was impossible to tell if the officers were on patrol.

Out of an abundance of caution, Nikki shoved her backpack under the seat and left it in the locked car. She had a permit to carry a concealed weapon but she didn't want any excuse to irritate Lara. Or Smitty.

She headed toward the locked gate, crossing a trail of hoof prints that cut the dry ground. A mechanism remotely opened the door but there was no buzzer to call for help, and a small sign noted the phone and location of the closest police station, emphasizing that visitors were discouraged. Yesterday, Lara had let Nikki in through the side gate, but no one was expecting her today and the area was deserted, driving home the difficulties of interviewing reticent cops.

Nikki pressed Lara's phone number but it went directly to voice mail. She waved at the surveillance camera, even tried rattling the mesh. But long minutes dragged by and clearly she was being ignored. Someone would eventually walk out and collect their vehicle but that could take hours.

Sighing, she eyed the brush beside the fence. The chaparral and sage scrub had been recently trimmed but there were still some spots where people could remain concealed, explaining why Billy had been the only one caught on camera. It also gave her an idea.

She picked her way around the perimeter, pausing to take pictures of the mesh, the surveillance camera and the shrubs—pretending to be totally engrossed—guessing that after Radar's assault the police would be super sensitive about security. Especially in the area where Billy had run up to the fence and lobbed the fire bomb.

Almost immediately an officer burst through the back door. His round face was familiar and she realized he was the young cop seated with Smitty at the bar.

"What are you doing?" he called, striding over to the gate. "Are you a lawyer?"

"No, I'm a private investigator. Nikki Drake." She pushed her business card between the mesh and then held her ID up to the fence, politely waiting for him to scan her credentials. "I'm looking for Billy Tanner," she added, "and just have a couple more questions."

"Sgt. Smith isn't here. He'll be back on Monday."

She flashed the officer her most charming smile. "It's actually my friend Lara I wanted to see."

"All right," the office said, walking over to the security box and jabbing in a code. "Come on in. She's cleaning stalls and will be happy for a break."

Nikki wasn't so sure of that but gave a vigorous nod, as if confident of her welcome.

"Heard you're looking for Billy," the officer said, waiting until the door closed behind her. "Weird how he took off. I've been watching the downtown hangouts but he's keeping a low profile."

"He may not be in the city," Nikki said. "Bus surveillance shows him getting on and off a later route. One that puts him within a mile of his house."

"We didn't have that information," the officer said, slanting her a curious look. "Only that he didn't catch his regular ride. Maybe we should have dug a little deeper." He started to say something more, then seemed to think better of it.

Nikki slowed her steps. This cop was younger than Smitty and Lara, not as hardened. Or as wary. She wondered how long he'd last with the police.

"Do you receive all the missing person bulletins?" she asked, seizing the chance to press for more information.

"Sure. Billy's came in on Wednesday but we didn't worry too much. His grandmother calls a lot, always crying wolf." He grimaced. "She's filed four missing reports on the other Tanner boy. But they found Jack every time, cruising the streets."

"Billy is apparently a much different kid than Jack."

"No doubt about that."

Movement flashed and Lara appeared, pushing a loaded wheelbarrow through the doorway. She stopped when she spotted Nikki.

"Good morning, Nikki," she said, her voice cool. "Back again? You should have called first."

Nikki felt the officer beside her stiffen, alerted by Lara's tone. He muttered something and eased away, making a prudent getaway, but not before shooting Lara a look of apology.

Lara waited until he'd disappeared. "What do you want now?" she asked. "I thought you'd find Smitty at the Rusty Nail. He always goes there on Fridays."

"He was there," Nikki said. "But I have a couple more questions."

Lara pushed the wheelbarrow away from the door, and straightened, reluctantly releasing her grip on the handles. "Two minutes," she said. "I'm already behind with the stalls now that Billy quit."

"Now that he's missing."

"Why do investigators always think you know more than us?" Lara said, shaking her head. But she motioned for Nikki to follow her further away from the barn—hopefully a sign she intended to be helpful. And that she might provide information she didn't want anyone else to hear.

"What do you need now?" Lara murmured.

"Is it possible Smitty chewed out Billy? Maybe after everyone else had left? Enough that Billy didn't want to come back?"

Lara shook her head. "Maybe Smitty was resentful the first couple weeks. Set him up for some ribbing. But you saw Radar's injuries. Smitty's not the type to harbor grudges though and he wouldn't have been abusive. He's a pretty good supervisor."

"What about you?" Nikki asked. "I understand you also have a special bond with Radar. In fact you'd ridden him, until Smitty made you swap." She pulled in a deep breath. Justin and Lara were longtime friends and Nikki had received the information informally. But Billy's welfare was more important than tiptoeing around Lara's hurt feelings.

Lara's smile was paper-thin, as if she guessed where Nikki had received that information. "True," she said. "Radar was my mount. And Smitty is my boss. Like I told you yesterday, at first I wanted to throttle Billy."

Nikki gave an empathetic nod. "I know that I wanted to kill the man who shot Gunner."

"But you didn't," Lara said. "And neither did I." Her voice rose with genuine indignation.

Genuine enough that Nikki deemed it safe to cross Lara off her list. The woman had always been upfront with her emotions. Not only that, Justin was a first-class judge of character. Smitty was the unknown.

"Have you known Sgt. Smith long," Nikki asked, switching the subject and giving Lara a chance to regroup.

"Smitty transferred in about a year ago," Lara said. "Mainly because he wanted to be around horses instead of stuck in a patrol car. I know you're not giving up on this but you're wasting everyone's time. Smitty's a good guy. He uses his vacation to help with animal rescue as well as fundraisers. I even heard him talking to Billy about the fall police auction, asking for ideas. They sometimes shared pizza. So you see, Smitty was *nice* to him."

Nikki gave an agreeable nod but she couldn't overlook Smitty's evasiveness about the bus. "I just want to ask him a couple more questions," she said, "before I drive out to the Tanners. What time does he usually arrive?"

"Smitty's not working this weekend. He covered the last one." Lara lifted a skeptical eyebrow. "You really think this is worth chasing? Considering the Tanner history? You don't think Billy ran away?"

"No," Nikki said. "I don't."

CHAPTER TEN

Nikki's car bounced over the faded blacktop and she slowed to a crawl, noting that the only two vehicles she'd met had been a pickup and a diesel-spewing tractor. Little wonder. The road curved like a snake, dotted with potholes and persistent weeds that poked through the cracks. Twice her little car had scraped its frame, prompting a muttered curse.

There didn't seem to be much of a tax base to justify road repairs. Most of the houses she'd passed simply struggled to remain upright, their sagging roofs proving their owners had fled to greener pastures. Earlier she'd spotted a bounding deer, its flashing white tail warning that animals used this back road as much as humans.

This was not a hospitable terrain. It reminded her of a recent search, when Gunner had led them to the body of a teenage rider. And it felt like she'd been driving for hours. Rubber stained one of the few straight stretches showing where locals had been drag racing. But now it was deserted. She topped another hill then pulled over to check the map on her phone screen, anticipating service would soon turn spotty.

Fortunately she hadn't overdriven. Two more miles and the Doberman kennel should be on her right. Then if she cut northeast over the hills, she'd cross a gravel road which would take her to the Tanners' house.

She continued her lonely drive, struck by how much she missed seeing Gunner's head in her rearview mirror. She'd always thought she could look after herself but his absence left her feeling off kilter. And vulnerable.

She was so caught up in her thoughts, she almost missed the sign announcing Shebib Breeding and Boarding Kennel. She braked and wheeled up the narrow driveway, pleasantly surprised at the lack of potholes. The gravel drive was smoother than the pitted blacktop, and her hardy car didn't drag once.

The gravel led to a ranch style home set close to the trees. The surrounding grass was brown and sun baked, mixed with scraggly weeds. She didn't hear any barking but there was plenty of canine evidence, judging by the wire kennels set back beside an old horse barn.

Leaning back in her seat, she turned off the ignition and glanced around. The entire property looked tired. The house needed painting and the only vehicle in the yard was older than her Subaru. Patches of dirt were dotted with yellow dandelions, dried grass and abandoned dog bones, bleached to a skeletal white.

She took several pictures of the buildings, car and kennels but remained in her car, waiting for the owner to appear. She knew better than to annoy a pack of protective Dobermans. This was one instance when it was probably good Gunner wasn't with her.

Dogs wheeled in their kennels, eyeing her car, but obviously they were locked up. Not a single animal charged toward her. From this distance, they didn't even appear to be Dobermans, but some sort of hunting dogs with long dangling ears. Bird dogs were usually friendly, she decided, so she opened her door and stepped out.

A warm nose pressed into the back of her leg. Her heart slammed against her ribs and she wheeled. But it wasn't a dog challenging her presence, just a pot-bellied pig. He had mottled skin, a dirt-smeared face and greeted her with friendly grunts.

"Hey, buddy," she said, bending and giving his head a scratch. "Are you the welcoming committee?"

"That's Porker," a man called, striding toward her. "He's my daughter's 4-H project. Great for keeping a dog property clean too. Are you with the police?"

"Working with them," she said, edging away from the pig and his odor, realizing now that his nose was coated, not with dirt, but dog feces. "Detective Decker asked me to stop by and pick up a package."

She passed the man her business card, surprised at how he'd materialized so quickly. The front door hadn't opened and he hadn't come from the kennels. She scanned the barn, noting the closed side door.

"I'm Tyson Shebib," he said, tucking her card into his back pocket. "Glad the police finally sent someone. I've been gathering material for the last eighteen months. It's criminal how the judge blackballed me. Such a pompous ass, insisting he be called 'Judge' just to remind everyone of his influence."

He paused, seeming to remember the man's grisly mutilation. "It's a shame what happened though. He did breed good-looking dogs. And I always liked his wife."

Nikki gave an encouraging nod, letting the man roll on. He seemed the type who liked to bare his soul, an investigator's dream.

"I've gathered records of all the show results," Tyson went on. "Going back six years. That along with puppy prices. He was so biased I guess someone finally blew their stack. Understandable. Because when a Doberman like my Czar and his progeny can't place in a show, it's clear something is wrong."

Nikki glanced at the mesh kennels. "I see you raise other dogs besides Dobermans."

Tyson's mouth twisted with grim humor. "No, Dobies only. But maybe their appearance isn't what you're used to. Want to walk back and take a look?"

"Definitely. Do you mind if I take some pictures?"

"Not at all. Take whatever you want. I'll let the dogs out." He was already striding toward the kennels, the pig trotting merrily behind him.

She pressed several pictures: the house, the barn, the woods. Even the pig. Then she hurried after Tyson, knowing it was safer to be close to him when the gates were opened. She didn't want his dogs assuming she was an uninvited guest.

On the other hand, they looked much less imposing than any Doberman she'd ever seen, more like some type of hound or perhaps a Weimaraner. It was their dangling ears and long tails that altered their appearance. Their tails curved over their backs, whipping back and forth in anticipation of being freed, making them seem totally approachable.

Tyson unlatched the kennel doors, one at a time. A few dogs paused to give her hand a curious sniff, but most just ran around them in excited circles. One black and tan Doberman stopped to play some sort of game with the pig and a muscular red dog raced off, scooping up a bone before loping toward the trees.

"They're great family pets," Tyson said, gesturing proudly at the pack of dogs. "We've had many excel in obedience and agility trials. It's the cropped ears and docked tails that make them look so intimidating. But I prefer the natural look. Especially if they're not in protection or law enforcement."

"It's astounding the difference it makes," Nikki said.

"Yes, but this appearance hasn't found much favor with the judges," Tyson said. "And Judge Kirby's disdain was a death blow for our small kennel. Even the boarders stopped coming. The man was an ass and he got worse every year. It's only going to help everyone that he's gone. Business has already picked up—"

He clamped his mouth shut, as if wanting to say more but reluctant to talk too poorly about the dead. Or more likely he remembered that the police were still looking for the killer.

"When did you last see the judge?" Nikki asked, relieved he'd brought up the subject.

"A long time ago," Tyson muttered.

Nikki didn't say a word, waiting him out.

"I guess it was at the LA show," he added, dipping his head and kicking the dirt with the toe of his boot. "At least four months back."

"Did you know him well?"

"Not really. He was a media hound. Only talked to me when he wanted something." Tyson smiled but it was devoid of humor. "The truth is he resented our business because we didn't conform to his breed standards. Was really vocal about it. He was a flamboyant man with a lot of influence so the damage was irreparable."

And the judge is dead, Nikki thought, feeling a swell of suspicion. Justin had asked for pictures but he'd thrown that request out more as an afterthought. He hadn't seemed to think Tyson was anything more than an envious competitor. But maybe there was something else going on.

She had a couple of hours before her one o'clock appointment with Mrs. Tanner, plenty of time to poke around. It would be great to find a nugget of information that would help police crack the case.

Tyson obviously blamed the judge for his struggling business. It seemed like a stretch but people had killed for less. And he had plenty of thick woods to hide a body. On the other hand, it would be folly to bury anything close to a dog kennel, not with a pack of canines eager to dig it up. She'd witnessed how quickly Gunner could sniff out human remains.

Maybe that wasn't a Doberman's strength though. She'd only watched the breed being trained in a protection role at the K9 center. And while they were dynamic on the agility and obedience courses, she couldn't remember how they had fared on scent exercises.

"Do Dobermans have good noses?" she asked.

"Sure, all dogs do." Tyson brightened, more relaxed talking about animals than the judge. "They're not as good as a bloodhound but they can hold their own. In fact, Czar—that's the red and tan dog chewing the bone—earned all three levels in the AKC scent tracking trials."

"Impressive," Nikki said, her gaze on Czar. "He seems interested in something beside the barn. Should we go over?"

"Sure. The dogs love tearing around the woods. Care for a walk?"

"Absolutely," she said. She missed her hikes with Gunner and this would also give her a chance to look around. Tyson shot toward the barn with such enthusiasm it was obvious he had nothing to hide there.

"Let's try the woods on the other side," she said. "Where there's more shade."

Tyson changed direction without any hesitation. The dogs and pig followed, in a cohesive pack, delighted about a run in the woods. One of the younger dogs gave an excited yip but other than that, their movement was quiet and efficient, marked only by the sound of crackling brush.

It was an odd group. Tyson appeared totally in his element, calling cheerfully to Czar and the other dogs while ordering the pig to go home. His bitter expression, so evident when he spoke about the judge, had disappeared, leaving him looking much younger.

"Let's hope Porker turns back," he said, grinning over his shoulder at Nikki. "The last couple weeks he's been gaining weight at almost two pounds a day, and my daughter, Katarina, will be annoyed if he burns it all off."

He went on to talk about the benefits of the 4-H program and how Katarina was also using Porker for a secondary school project. Apparently cleaning up after the dogs was her job, but the pig had more or less taken over that duty. And Katarina was delighted.

"Now not all swine will eat dung," Tyson added. "But Porker isn't picky. He loves that most of my dogs are on a raw food diet."

He launched into the pros and cons of various diets and breeds before Nikki had a chance to steer the subject back to the judge. Tyson's opinions were interesting though and she was keen to learn more. Her mother had been allergic so they'd never owned pets of any kind, and Nikki felt she had a lot of ground to make up.

Considering Tyson's flexibility about their direction of walk, he had nothing sinister to conceal. Besides, back in her apprentice days it had been drummed into her psyche that investigators learned more if they just took their time and went with the flow.

So she relaxed and listened and simply enjoyed the pleasure of a companionable dog walk.

Forty minutes later, they had circled the property and emerged from the woods on the west side of the kennels, a totally stress-free walk for both humans and canines. She helped him lock up the dogs, patting them goodbye and remembering all their names except for the small one with the rust-colored tail. The sparkling water bowls and overall cleanliness of the runs was most impressive. Whether it was Tyson's, Katarina's or Porker's doing, these Dobermans had a healthy and caring home.

And the visit had been more fun than work. She'd even told Tyson a bit about Gunner. While it had been bittersweet to have other dogs frolicking at her side, she now knew more about the cutthroat world of dog shows...as well as the names and addresses of all the breeders the judge had allegedly blackballed. She'd also had the pleasure of observing the Dobermans' strength and obedience, and why Tyson abhorred the practice of ear cropping.

"Thank you for your time," she said, opening her hatchback and making room for Tyson's three cardboard boxes. "I really enjoyed the visit."

"Maybe you can come out with your Shepherd," Tyson said. "I'm sure Gunner will be running around again. Dogs are amazingly resilient."

He was one of the few people who showed much optimism, and she gave him a grateful smile as she moved around to the driver's side. It was then that she spotted the teenage girl standing on the porch.

"Hey, Katarina," Tyson called, his arms wrapped around a bulging cardboard box. "Come meet Nikki. She's with the police."

Nikki didn't bother to correct him. She was too busy trying not to stare. Katarina was stunningly beautiful with shiny brown hair and pink, pouty lips. She wore faded jeans and an oversized T-shirt that read: Doberman Security. She didn't look much older than fourteen. And she was heavily pregnant.

"Hi, Katarina," Nikki said. "Nice kennel you have here."

"Thanks. I try to keep it clean. Did you meet all the dogs? And Porker?"

"Sure did. Good luck with your project."

Katarina shuffled to the top of the steps. "Yes, but it sucks that he's doing so well and the weigh-in dates have changed. It gives everyone else time to catch up."

Nikki made a sympathetic sound but she couldn't remember what Tyson had said about the 4-H dates. Perhaps she hadn't listened, not wanting to think too closely about the end game for the friendly pig. Besides, she couldn't linger if she were to be on time for the Tanner appointment, especially considering the state of these roads.

"Is that Judge Kirby's stuff?" Katarina's voice rose as she stared into the open hatchback. "Are you going to help me collect my last pay check? I put my time sheet in one of the boxes so the police could see all my hours."

"You worked for Judge Kirby?"

Katarina gave a mournful nod. "Scrubbed his crates, washed and walked his dogs, did all the grunt work. But he never paid me for the last show." Her voice rose an octave. "And it was a three-day weekend."

"How long did you work for him?"

"Two years, off and on."

Nikki edged toward the bottom of the steps, close enough that she could smell Katarina's floral shampoo. "Is the judge's kennel close by?" Nikki asked. "Did you go there after school?"

Katarina gave an impatient headshake, her shiny hair swinging over her shoulders. "No. It's close to San Francisco but we often went to the same shows. He brought a lot of dogs, and he and his wife always needed help. So, are the police going to help me get my money?"

"I'm a private investigator," Nikki said. "I'm not with the police. But their focus is finding out what happened to Judge Kirby. It's not about employment matters. Did you contact the judge's wife? She'd probably know your hours better than anyone else."

Katarina crossed her arms, her expression sullen. She looked a lot like her father when he'd first talked about the judge. "His wife is too upset to talk to me," she muttered.

"That's understandable. She's going through a tough time. But does she have a kennel manager? An assistant? There must be someone who knew how hard you worked."

"Forget it. This whole thing sucks." Katarina turned, yanked open the door, slamming it with a note of finality.

Tyson joined Nikki at the bottom of the porch. If he was surprised by his daughter's abrupt disappearance, he didn't show it.

"There," he said, rubbing his hands in satisfaction. "Now everyone can see what was going on. The judge didn't care about the dogs, only about lining his own pockets and lording it over everyone else. I don't know who killed him and I can't prove he took kickbacks. But I think plenty of people had axes to grind."

"Yes," Nikki said. "I think you're right."

CHAPTER ELEVEN

Nikki eased her car to a stop as soon as she was out of sight of Tyson's house then dictated the details of her visit into her phone. Police appreciated a comprehensive report and she wanted to note everything while the observations were fresh, and correct. She'd worked part-time as a clerk in an investigator's office and, at the age of sixteen, had learned the hard way that one never knew when notes would be relied on in court.

Next, she called Justin. His phone went directly to voicemail. She left a brief message then pressed back against her headrest, sickened by her suspicions. She liked Tyson and didn't want him to be guilty of anything. In fact, she'd nearly driven away viewing him as a victim.

But was Judge Kirby the father of Katarina's unborn baby? Would that be sufficient motive for Tyson? He'd been very blunt about how much he despised the process of ear cropping and the unnecessary pain it caused the puppies. According to social media, the judge hadn't been a nice man. Some reports had labeled him a womanizing egomaniac. Yet killing the man and cutting off his ears?

The thought made her grimace.

Her cell buzzed and she grabbed it, anticipating Justin's return call. But it was Sonja.

"I just listened to your message," Sonja said. "You're cancelling coffee again? I assume you're helping that woman from yesterday. Thought you would."

"You did?" Nikki straightened so fast her knee slammed the steering wheel. She rubbed her leg, calming her voice. Ever since Sonja proved she truly had psychic ability, Nikki tended to read too much into her words. Still, maybe she knew something.

"So, did you pick up something when you spoke to my client?" Nikki asked, hopeful but cautious. "Do you know where Billy is? Is he safe?"

"Actually our conversation was more about the wisdom of waiting outside your office. I know she doesn't like dogs. She views them as a farm animal, not worth feeding unless they have a purpose. That was the reason I wasn't sure you'd take her case."

"You could sense all that?"

"No, she told me," Sonja said, laughing.

"Oh." Nikki sighed, her disappointment escaping in that single word. It would have been wonderful if Sonja could confirm Billy was safe and sleeping in the woods. Nikki's more rational side believed that good investigative work always trumped a psychic. She always felt a little uncomfortable with her friend's spiritual side. Still, Sonja had been right before.

"Well," Nikki said, keeping her voice light. "Maybe you could do some of your hokey pokey stuff and help me out?"

"Are you paying me?" Sonja asked. "Because I don't believe you'll charge Mrs. Tanner for much more than your expenses. And unlike you, I don't work for free."

Nikki gave a reluctant smile. She had no compunction about billing law firms for her work, but people like Mrs. Tanner brought back aching memories of her own family's struggles. And she knew big-hearted Sonja would understand.

"You're right," Nikki admitted. "There won't be much money in it. But how about I buy you dinner if you help me find Billy?"

"It's a deal. But how are you feeling? You've met with his grandmother. What do your instincts say?"

"That he needs help." Nikki spoke so quickly it surprised her.

Clearly it surprised Sonja too. She didn't speak for a moment. "Well, there's your answer," Sonja said. "I think you're finally opening up and listening to your inner voice."

Nikki didn't think she had much of an inner voice. She was more of a black and white person. Any extrasensory perception came from Gunner. And he was out of action, for now.

"I'm heading to the Tanners," she said. "What if I picked up an item of Billy's? Could you look at it for me? Run your magic?"

"It's not magic."

"Well, it's magic to me," Nikki said. "And I mean that as a compliment."

"That's progress, I suppose," Sonja said. "Make sure to bring me one of Billy's favorite things. And for payment we're going to an expensive restaurant, not Vinny's where you get everything for free. The restaurant won't even have to be dog friendly, at least not for a couple more weeks."

"What do you mean?" Nikki gripped her phone a little tighter. "Are you saying Gunner will be well enough to come home soon? Do you see that?"

"I see that you're worrying about him," Sonja said. "Worrying unnecessarily. I have to go now. A client wants to book a widows' party where they all talk to their dead husbands. Those are always interesting."

Nikki cradled the silent phone for a long moment, warmed with relief. Sonja had been a loyal friend ever since she'd rented the office space next to Nikki. Other than Justin, she'd been the first person to meet Gunner. Sonja kept homemade dog treats in her office, housed an assortment of rescue animals on her little farm—including Nikki's pony—and totally understood Nikki's love for Gunner. So her statement that Nikki was "worrying unnecessarily" had to mean something good. Sonja was the best psychic Nikki knew.

Sonja was also the only psychic she knew, but right now it helped to hear encouraging feedback. Her friend would never have said anything if she wasn't optimistic about Gunner's prognosis. And that lifted Nikki's spirits considerably. Even the narrow country road seemed less desolate. She eased her car onto the cracked blacktop and continued east, smiling as she drove.

When her phone buzzed minutes later, she was still floating in good humor.

"You sound happy," Justin said. "Did you break my case?"

The fact that he didn't seem to be joking gave her another lift. Justin always had faith in her abilities. He'd been her biggest supporter ever since she was a kid working for him at a local riding stable. Recently he'd turned into much more than a friend, and of course, he'd given her Gunner. For that alone, she'd be forever in his debt. And she'd love to help blow open the case.

"I might have found something," she said. "Did you know Tyson's teenage daughter worked for the judge at dog shows?"

"Not until I listened to your message. Wait a moment."

She heard him tell someone about putting a rush on prints. When he returned to the phone, his voice was a bit impatient. "It's doubtful the daughter had anything to do with abducting the judge," he said. "And slicing off body parts. Our profilers suggest a non-Hispanic white male, blue collar, physically strong—"

"She's pregnant, Justin."

Justin blew out a breath, slow and thoughtful. "And her father fits the profile and already is bitter. Think he did it?"

"Not really. He definitely blamed the judge for his struggling business. Says it's already improving. But I don't see him as a killer. I've been wrong before though." *And recently.*

"That was different," Justin said quickly. "You were too close. I'll get out to Tyson's place," he went on. "Have a chat with him."

Nikki didn't envy the man. Justin's "chats" were never fun. It had been a while since Justin had turned that searing stare on her, but when he did, she wanted to babble every thought in her head.

"How long were you there?" Justin asked.

"A couple hours," she said. "He showed me his kennels. We took the Dobermans for a hike. Beautiful dogs."

"Well done. I knew you'd be the best person for the job."

His praise surprised her. It also left her feeling guilty since they both knew the job would be used to reduce Mrs. Tanner's mileage. "I only picked up some boxes," Nikki said. "It was a coincidence I even met Katarina. She stepped out of the house just as I was leaving."

"That's my point. I don't have any officers interested in dogs. Or beautiful, observant ones that Tyson would want to spend time with."

"So I wasn't hired just so you could send a paying gig my way?"

"No," he said.

She digested that for a moment, somewhat deflated. "That's good...I guess. I thought you were being nice."

"I'm not that nice."

"Right," she said. "I have to go. I'm almost at the Tanners' house."

"Wait," Justin said, his voice rich with humor. "Are you going to the K9 center or will you be coming home tonight?"

Home. The fact that he didn't call it his house smoothed the fact that he hadn't hired her to be nice. And of course, she didn't want special favors. She just needed to know that he cared.

"Yes, I'll be sticking around until I find Billy."

"Good," he said.

CHAPTER TWELVE

Smitty gunned his truck down one of the few straight stretches and checked the time. He met Ray Gibson by the farm gate every third Saturday. Today though, he was a few minutes late.

He pulled onto the rutted gravel at the bottom of Ray's narrow driveway. Ray wasn't in sight and, as usual, the gate was locked.

Ray worked for the county, picking up animal carcasses from the side of the road. He also provided temporary refuge for animals removed from neglectful owners, and Smitty liked to help him whenever he could. Five years ago, someone had tried to reclaim a pair of abused hogs. Now a high steel mesh fence protected the entrance, keeping the property safe from trespassers. Smitty had helped pour the concrete.

He grabbed the coffee he'd brought. Stepped out, lowered his tailgate and carefully set down the two cups.

"Morning," Ray said, his voice soft and gentle.

Smitty glanced around. He hadn't even heard the man approach. "Good morning, Ray. Got the hay you wanted." He gestured at the alfalfa bales. "And your coffee."

"Is that the kind of hay you feed Radar?" Ray asked, resting his hip against the tailgate and gratefully accepting the coffee.

Smitty nodded. Ray always showed keen interest in his horse and in all of the organization's rescue animals. A month ago, the gentle man had sobbed when Smitty told him about a dog that had died after being found tethered to a railing. His owner had neglected to leave the animal food or water while on a hot date that had extended into a Tuesday.

"So Radar's healing well?" Ray asked.

Smitty nodded, taking a long sip of coffee, now lukewarm and easy to drink.

"What percentage of his back was burned?"

"Too much," Smitty said, his hand tightening around the cup. He wanted to enjoy his weekend off. Not talk about Radar's back and agonize if the horse would be able to carry his weight again. Possibly Radar would do better with Lara. She was much lighter and would be delighted to have her old partner back. She'd been so cooperative about working with the new mounts that she deserved to have her pick.

"Don't worry," Ray said. "The person who did it will be punished."

"Yeah," Smitty muttered. "That kid put in some long hours. But I guess he didn't like horses as much as he pretended. He ran off last week. The court isn't going to like that."

Smitty knew he shouldn't take Billy's defection personally but he'd thought the kid felt genuinely bad about Radar. Smitty had even considered applying to keep him on and creating a paying job. Billy didn't talk much about his home life but it was apparent his grandmother struggled just to put groceries on the table. Hardworking families like that could use a little help.

"I share your outrage, brother." Ray reached out and gripped Smitty's shoulder. "Animals deserve a life free from exploitation."

Smitty took another swig of coffee, fighting his irritation. Ray's extremist comments often got on his nerves. He had little tolerance for placard-waving prattle. And he definitely didn't like the man's touch.

He could better accept the familiarity if Ray were a beautiful redhead...like Nikki Drake. He'd checked her out on his computer last night and learned she was legitimate. Had put in her apprentice hours and earned her license. That had calmed him. She was only doing her job, chasing him down at the Rusty Nail, asking legitimate questions.

Now, on this sunny Saturday, he found her suspicions more amusing than threatening. He actually gave her points for having the nerve to check out his truck. She was intelligent, brave and smelled good, unlike Ray who always carried a rather unpleasant cloud of barn odors. And the man was still squeezing his shoulder, as if they were brothers in arms.

"Dammit, Ray." Smitty forced a chuckle as he pivoted away from the man. "When are you going to slaughter those hogs?"

"Never," Ray said, his voice reproachful. "I'd never hurt an animal. They're family now."

Smitty sighed. He often dropped off hay and grain, and the county provided a feed allowance for rescues, but hogs were big eaters. Ray must be digging into his own pockets to keep them healthy. "How many are you looking after?" he asked.

"Sixteen," Ray said. "But I supplement their food with road kill. Pigs are indiscriminate eaters. They love carcasses, especially when they're fresh."

Smitty's gaze lowered over the dark spatter on the man's boots. Ray must have dashed down after carving up food for the pigs. The thought was rather repulsive. So was the pungent smell of organ meat.

He dumped the remainder of his coffee on the gravel and tossed his cup into the back of his truck, suddenly in a hurry to leave. This wasn't a pleasant topic for his weekend off. He craved space. And fresh air.

"Want me to drive you up before I go?" he asked, not surprised when Ray shook his head. Smitty always offered but Ray never liked to cut into anyone's time. And Smitty appreciated that.

"I'll come down and pick up the bales later," Ray said. He stared at Smitty, his dark eyes intent. "And don't worry about Radar's torturer. He'll regret his cruelty."

Smitty stepped into his truck with a non-committal grunt, waved and pulled the door shut. All this talk about Billy left him feeling guilty. He hadn't been entirely truthful when questioned by the investigator last night. Hadn't wanted to admit he'd left Billy unsupervised last Saturday. He certainly didn't want the brass to find out.

But dammit, he'd trusted the kid. Had been totally shocked when Billy ran off. Now though, Nikki Drake's questions left him more worried than pissed. What if she was right and Billy hadn't chosen to ghost?

He drove a few more miles, warring with his conscience. Then he veered right, pulling into the parking lot of Lena's, the local general store. The store offered two fuel pumps and one of them was diesel. He didn't need gas but it was one of the higher spots where his cell phone didn't drop calls. And he had to make things right, for Billy's sake.

He plucked Nikki Drake's business card from his wallet and propped it against the steering wheel. She might not answer and he certainly wasn't going to leave a message. Maybe he wouldn't have to talk to her yet. He punched in her number before he could change his mind.

She answered immediately and, like him, was obviously driving. Music rippled in the background. He wished now he'd thought a little more about what he would say, how he'd slide in the information without looking like an idiot. Or a liar.

"It's Aaron Smith, Smitty," he said, keeping his voice casual. Unofficial.

"Hi, Smitty," she said, sounding just as relaxed. She was making it easy for him, he thought. Even though he hadn't been cooperative last night, trying to run her off. Of course, his intimidation hadn't worked. It had only alerted her enough to snoop around his truck. Kudos to her.

He cleared his throat. "I've been thinking about last Saturday. The day Billy Tanner disappeared."

"Yes," she said, her music no longer audible.

"Now that I've checked your credentials," he said. "I feel better about discussing the details."

"Of course," she said.

He hesitated, hoping this wouldn't cost him his badge. However, he'd had more time to think. And her fears about Billy left him concerned. "There's a possibility Billy stayed a little after five last Saturday night. He might have left closer to seven. I stepped out for a couple hours when he was closing up. Just thought you should know."

There was no sound. Three crows hopped around a metal dumpster, searching for tidbits, but Smitty couldn't hear their caws. He was too focused on Nikki, listening for her breathing, wondering if she was still there.

Finally she spoke. "I learned he took the late bus that evening," she said. "Now we know why. Your information helps fill in that missing gap. Do you think he stayed at the barn until seven?"

"Probably," he said, relieved her tone was more curious than accusing. She must have seen the police report. Noticed the glaring omission. But she wasn't jumping on him. Was even using the term "we" as if they were in it together.

"Billy was worried about Radar's itching," he added. "He wanted to stay and see if a new ointment would help. But he wasn't upset or anything."

"So you didn't personally see Billy after five o'clock?"

"Correct," Smitty said. And even though he'd just admitted to a huge security breach, a weight lifted from his shoulders.

"Okay, thanks. I appreciate your call." She promised to update him with any new information and cut the connection, sounding more concerned about Billy than aghast at how he'd left the kid unsupervised.

Smitty dragged a hand over his jaw, his thoughts wrapped around Billy. Maybe Mrs. Tanner's concern was justified and her grandson hadn't run off. Maybe that hadn't been Billy he'd seen by the mall. At least someone was looking into it, even if it was a lone investigator with limited resources. There wasn't much Nikki could do on her own. But that was going to change. He'd make sure of it.

He wheeled his truck out of the lot, in a hurry now. He'd drive to the station and make an official push for more action. He also knew every animal organization in the county. They were always ready to post lost pet pictures and would be keen to help find a local teen. Their volunteers would have social media buzzing. His superiors wouldn't have to know it came from him. He should have put this in motion earlier instead of resenting Billy for breaking his trust.

His tires squealed as he careened around a sharp corner. A blur of brown leaped from the ditch. *Thump*. He didn't have time to brake, only caught panicked eyes and a flash of white as a deer ricocheted off his bumper.

He jerked to a stop and checked the rearview mirror. A crumpled heap lay motionless, splayed near the middle of the road.

"Aw, hell." Groaning, he backed up, stepped from his truck and checked the deer. A plump young doe in her prime, now very dead, just another unfortunate animal for Ray to collect.

He checked his phone. But there were no bars, just the dreaded "no service" message. He'd leave the doe on the side of the road and call Ray later with the location. Hopefully the man would pick her up today on his rounds.

He circled the front of his pickup, stooping to check the damage. Not much, just a cracked grill and a shiny spot where the deer had rubbed dust off the bumper. He straightened, sighing with regret.

The doe had shot unexpectedly from the brush, but he'd been driving too fast, thinking of Billy and not the road. Unfortunately she had paid the price. A moment ago, she'd been a picture of grace and beauty. Now she was a twisted carcass stiffening beneath the sun. Already flies circled, drawn by the blood trickling from her nostrils. More scavengers would appear soon, eager to feast on her body.

Smitty sighed again and lowered his tailgate. He'd never been one to drive past, leaving animals on the road to rot, and this one was his responsibility. Besides, it was only a short detour back to Ray's, and the man would be appreciative.

Fifteen minutes later, Smitty wheeled back onto the gravel at the bottom of Ray's treed driveway. The hay bales still sat by the closed gate.

He dragged the deer off the back of his truck and positioned her behind the hay, out of sight of passing cars. Scant traffic used this road, but he didn't want to cause Bambi nightmares for any children.

Already her body was changing. Fleas visibly scattered, leaving their host as her body cooled. Grimacing, he stepped back, wishing his phone worked here so he could alert Ray. Carcasses deteriorated fast in the California sun, and she should be collected and gutted soon.

He glanced once more at the deer then at the locked gate. It was possible to walk around the fence if one didn't mind squeezing through some ugly brush. After about twenty feet, the mesh stopped and he could loop back onto the driveway. It wouldn't take a whole lot of time to walk up and find Ray.

Sighing, he pushed into the woods surrounding the locked gate. The underlying brush was even thicker than he remembered, and he had to bend much more than his back liked. Brambles tugged at his shirt, scratching his skin, but he bulled forward, accepting the thorns as his penance. He angled a sharp right, guessing by now he was well clear of the mesh barrier. When he crashed from the woods, he was on the gravel on the other side of the gate.

Tugging off a stubborn briar and wiping pinpoints of blood from his arms he began the hot trudge up the driveway. This shouldn't take more than ten minutes and no doubt Ray would be happy to see him, grateful to have an unexpected supply of fresh meat.

After all, pigs were always hungry.

CHAPTER THIRTEEN

"These biscuits are delicious," Nikki said, lifting a second one off the plate. She wasn't an enthusiastic cook but she appreciated good food. And these biscuits were light and flaky and seemed to melt in her mouth.

"Fill your boots." Mrs. Tanner pushed a chipped butter dish closer to Nikki. "You're the first person to take the time to drive out here since Billy disappeared. The cops never bothered. "

"The police are very busy," Nikki murmured, trying to keep her lips from smacking in delight. She couldn't remember when she'd tasted such fantastic biscuits.

"But my taxes pay for policing," Mrs. Tanner complained. "And they haven't done a thing. On television, cops always visit the house and look around. Of course, Jack might have refused to let them in." She glanced over her shoulder, looking through a spotless window decorated by frilly yellow curtains and a handmade sun catcher. "He doesn't like the police much."

Nikki gave an encouraging nod, her mouth too full to talk. Besides, she was curious about Billy's brother and it was wiser to let Mrs. Tanner vent. Nikki had already heard the woman's opinion of Jack's probation officer, but she could sift through that conversation later, searching for any nugget of information. The most inconsequential detail might be the one to help find Billy. Men generally opened up with a little flattery but women often just needed people to listen. To know that someone else cared.

"Jack doesn't like the Social Services people either," Mrs. Tanner went on. "They keep threatening to take him. But he's kept his nose clean for the past five months."

"It must be a challenge." Nikki pulled her eyes off the plate of biscuits, reluctantly resolving not to eat a third. "Raising two teenage boys."

"Billy was easy. He takes after his mom. But Jack is like his father, God rest their souls." She straightened the butter knife so it was more properly aligned on the edge of the plate. "The boys may look alike but Billy has always been the gentle one. Sparky hasn't stopped pining since he left. Just lies there like a useless lump."

"May I talk to Jack?" Nikki asked, glancing out the window to where a dark-haired teenager angrily split wood.

Angrily. Nikki didn't like how that word jumped into her head. But Jack's body language was unmistakable. Tension corded his wiry shoulders, and he ignored the small brown-and-white dog who watched with mournful eyes.

"I'll ask him to come in," Mrs. Tanner said, reaching for her cane. "He's wary of authority. So don't expect much."

"No need to interrupt him yet," Nikki said, knowing it would be easier to check the house while Jack was outside. Not dogging her steps, watching her every move with hostile eyes. "First, I'd like to see Billy's room. And his computer."

"He doesn't have a computer. Just the shared one over there where he types his schoolwork. That's where he wrote his letter of apology. But like I said, we don't have internet service."

Nikki eyed the blocky computer. It looked like a relic from a local library and still had a "purge" sticker pasted on its side.

"Billy and Jack share a room," Mrs. Tanner went on. "And Jack won't want you poking around in there."

"But I might see something that will help find Billy."

"You won't find anything in there. Billy is a good boy. Jack is too...now. And I can't have you stirring up trouble, maybe siccing Child Services on us."

"I'm only here to find your grandson," Nikki said. But her suspicious mind was racing. Mrs. Tanner's concern about losing custody was troubling. The woman didn't seem strong enough to physically abuse anyone but Jack certainly was. The power in his body was obvious in the way he wielded the axe. Did the two of them have something to do with Billy running away? Maybe it wasn't Billy's work place that had prompted him to disappear. Perhaps it was his home life.

"I'd like to use your bathroom as well," Nikki added, not wanting Mrs. Tanner to dig in her heels. She wasn't the type to be pushed. But letting Nikki use the bathroom was a good first step.

"Help yourself." Mrs. Tanner peered out the window again, seemingly more concerned about Jack's movements than Nikki's. "The bathroom is the first door on the left. And while you're down there, Billy's room is across the hall. You can go in there if you're quick. It shouldn't take you long to look around. Jack doesn't have to know."

"Thank you," Nikki murmured, quickly rising from the table. Mrs. Tanner wanted her to hurry and she intended to heed the woman's advice.

The hall was less than fifteen feet long and seemed to run downhill. Nikki reached the bathroom in three long strides. She pushed open the door, stepped inside and locked the door. She didn't actually need to use the facilities but bathrooms were a treasure trove of information.

She peered around, noting that someone in the Tanner household had superior cleaning skills. Everything gleamed, from the faded beige floor tiles to the white toilet bowl. Three toothbrushes stood in a sparkling glass, alongside a tube of toothpaste neatly folded from the bottom. Three towels hung over a crooked rack. There were very few hiding places.

She turned on the tap, using the running water to hide the sounds of her lifting the lid of the toilet tank. Nothing there but water and the flush apparatus. Someone had recently replaced the orange bulb. She carefully replaced the lid then peeked in the cabinet above the sink.

For three people, the shelves were relatively sparse: toothpaste, razors, low-dose ASA, two bars of generic soap, and five bottles of prescription drugs. She picked up each bottle, scanning the dates and labels. All were prescribed to Elizabeth G. Tanner including a blood thinner, medication for gastric reflux, and an antibiotic for emphysema. There was also a container of muscle relaxant, long expired and barely used. Certainly there were no drugs on display for Billy, legal or otherwise.

She closed the cabinet and checked behind the shower curtain. Only soap, shampoo, and a well-scrubbed tub. Someone had recently added caulking around the faucet and the pristine walls glistened. Nothing more to be learned here other than the Tanners possessed enviable cleaning and handyman skills.

She turned off the running tap, flushed the toilet and peered out the window.

Jack was still chopping, scattering wood chips with the ferocity of his blows. Sparky had wisely retreated to his dog house. Only the tip of his nose was visible, and he pulled it back every time a wood chip flew too close. Other than that, the dog remained unmoving.

Nikki crossed the hall and stepped into Billy's room, relieved she'd have a few minutes alone. It shouldn't take long to look around. The room was tiny. Two single beds—made with military precision—occupied most of the floor space along with a dresser, one brown wooden chair and an ancient fan. The only window in the bedroom slid open so easily she suspected it also served as an exit.

The closet door was ajar and she eased it wider, glancing inside. There were two distinct sides, separated by a plastic pant rack. Jack seemed to have most of the hanger space, but that was probably because of age privilege rather than any type of abuse. His clothes were two sizes larger and typical street teen while Billy's clothes were mainly plaids and jeans, exactly like the photos Mrs. Tanner had provided. Nothing was out of place in the closet and Nikki found nothing tucked in their pockets or hidden in their shoes.

She moved to the dresser, listening for a cautious moment before edging open the drawers. Mrs. Tanner may have given her permission, but any self-respecting teen would resent a stranger poking around his underwear. On the other hand, Jack had spent time in juvenile detention so he was probably no stranger to random room checks.

Yet there wasn't anything of interest. Even after running her hand along the bottom of each drawer and checking both mattresses, she turned up nothing except a men's magazine.

Certainly no drugs, liquor, or anything to make fire bombs. This room was as empty of clues as Billy's social media footprint. Definitely nothing to suggest abuse or reasons to flee. Unfortunately there was also nothing to indicate where he might hole up if he had chosen to go to ground.

She backed up to the door, giving the room one last scan. Probably even Gunner wouldn't have been able to find anything here. Mrs. Tanner ran a tight ship and if Billy had something worth hiding, he must have kept it outside.

Her gaze drifted around the room then back to the fan. It wasn't plugged in and took up precious space. The California nights had been cool and likely the fan hadn't been needed for a while. It felt wrong.

Crouching down, she peered inside. Saw only four crooked paddles with surprisingly little dust. Metal clamps held the motor compartment in place. She pulled out a coin and pried open the back.

A plastic baggie dropped at her feet.

She scooped up the bag and inspected it by the window. Weird. Not powder or pills or edibles. It looked like dog biscuits: milk bones, the kind that came in the red box on the grocery store shelves. She opened the bag and gave it a cautious sniff. Yes, definitely dog bones. But why would someone hide dog food in their room? Was Billy starved for food?

Jack appeared well fed. He was lean and lanky but had plenty of muscle. Smitty and Lara had said nothing about Billy losing weight, but would they have noticed? Maybe Mrs. Tanner was punishing Billy for throwing the firebomb and causing potential attention from Child Services. And when he had run away, she'd felt so guilty that she'd hired Nikki.

On the other hand, what would stop Billy from getting up in the night and sneaking some food from the kitchen? Anything would be tastier than dog biscuits. Nothing in the room suggested restraints and there wasn't a lock on the door. But perhaps Jack was the enforcer. He was older and bigger, and no doubt had learned several intimidation methods while running with a gang.

Nikki left the room, stopping only to check the doorknob. It had no lock. And she'd already noted that the window would permit the exit of a flexible teen.

Mrs. Tanner was standing in front of the kitchen sink, hands deep in soapy water. She turned at Nikki's approach. "I don't imagine you found anything," she said. "The boys were brought up to be neat."

"Very neat," Nikki said, her gaze sweeping over the fridge and cupboards. There didn't appear to be any locking mechanisms but her suspicions were on high alert.

"I just need to grab a glass of water," she said, reaching up and opening a cupboard door. It opened easily, revealing cereal, crackers and rice.

"Not that cupboard," Mrs. Tanner said. "Glasses are to the right."

Nikki put on a show of struggling to find the correct cupboard and by the time she picked up a glass, it was obvious there was food readily available. And not a single lock.

"So what's your plan?" Mrs. Tanner asked as she took Nikki's glass, filled it with cold water and passed it back. "Where are you going now?"

"I want to retrace Billy's route after he got off the bus. But first I'd like to have Jack's input."

"All right. But he doesn't know anything or else he'd have found Billy himself. And he's been miserable. Barely comes inside except to sleep."

"Did the boys get along well?" Nikki asked, watching the woman's expression. "Was Billy having any problems at home? At school? With you?"

Mrs. Tanner's eyes widened with such incredulity it was impossible to believe the indignation in her voice wasn't real. "Of course not," she snapped. "Whatever happened is related to that police horse. I just know it!"

Nikki gave a soothing nod and pulled out her notebook. "I just want to check every angle. Can you tell me the name of his school? And his teachers?"

"Greenfield Consolidated," Mrs. Tanner muttered, her voice resentful. "I don't know the names of his teachers. There's a bunch of them."

"That's okay," Nikki said, jotting down the information. "I'll talk to the principal."

"Jack might know more of their names. But you're wasting your time. You should check out the cops where Billy worked. That's why I hired you, because the police weren't taking me seriously. I see you're not either."

The woman's eyes glittered with unshed tears and Nikki gentled her voice. "I just want to be thorough. We know Billy got off the bus. So something happened between your house and that last stop. I want to concentrate on this area, including what road Billy might have taken to go home."

She pulled out a satellite map, one of several she'd printed, and positioned it on the table. "It looks like there's a fire road that cuts through the woods," she said, tracing it with a finger. "Or else he might have followed the blacktop to where it splits right here. There's also a possibility he hitchhiked."

"Billy wouldn't hitchhike." Mrs. Tanner's voice shook with emotion. "He'd never take a ride from a stranger. And that old fire road is full of deadfalls. It wouldn't save any time."

"But there's a possibility?"

Mrs. Tanner wrung her hands, her eyes fixed on the map. "That bus wasn't his regular one so I can't really say. I hope he's not hurt and lying out in the cold, fighting off varmints."

Nikki gave the woman's shoulder a comforting squeeze and scooped up the map. "I'll just step outside," she said, "and see what Jack thinks."

"Wait a sec." Mrs. Tanner fumbled for a napkin. "Take him the rest of the biscuits. He's been so grumpy lately. Maybe they'll soften him up, put him in a helping frame of mind. I can make a fresh batch for when you find Billy."

Her tremulous smile tugged at Nikki's heart. The woman's devotion to her youngest grandson made it unlikely she'd ever harm him and Nikki was almost embarrassed by her earlier suspicions.

Jack, though, was another matter. Because Billy had ridden the bus to within a mile of his house. Something—or someone—had stopped him from coming home. And sibling rivalry could be a dangerous thing.

CHAPTER FOURTEEN

The screen door clicked behind Nikki as she stepped outside onto the Tanner's aging back porch. Three boards had recently been replaced and their light color contrasted with the rest of the wood. A clothesline ran from the top of the porch to a stout evergreen. Jeans dangled from the line along with an assortment of shirts and underwear. Rain barrels had been placed on both sides of the house as well as a smaller blue barrel next to the chicken coop.

She climbed down the steps and detoured around a vegetable garden with a drip hose running through the middle.

Sparky stepped from his dog house, his chain rattling a welcome, watching her approach with lively interest. Mrs. Tanner had complained of his barking but right now the dog was silent. He sat and waved a paw in the air, staring at the food in her hand with beseeching eyes.

"Your dog has a good nose," Nikki said, smiling at Jack. "Guess he smells the biscuits."

Jack just scowled, his hands gripping the axe, not nearly as friendly as the dog. The knuckles of both hands were reddened and his right hand was marked with puckered white skin. A tattoo extended below the sleeve of his black T-shirt, draping over well-defined muscles. If she'd spotted him in a city alley, she would have entered with caution.

"It's not surprising your dog wants one," Nikki went on, determined to soften his defenses. "Your grandmother is a wonderful cook."

Jack glowered, still not speaking. For a boy of sixteen, he was rather intimidating. She wondered what his role had been in the youth gang. His right hand looked jagged white against the tan of his skin. And the skin on his hands was thickened from numerous scrapes.

She had to give him bonus points for Sparky's behavior though. If the dog had been afraid of Jack, he would be cowering in his dog house, not looking bright-eyed at the food. That knowledge was comforting and it proved the dog might be a conversation starter. Few people could resist talking about their pet.

"It looks like he wants me to shake his paw," Nikki said, ignoring Jack's hostility. She would have felt better if he put down the axe but they weren't at that point yet. "May I give him a piece of biscuit?"

Jack didn't answer.

"My dog, Gunner, looks at me like that when he wants a treat," she said. "He doesn't raise his paw though. He doesn't know many tricks."

"Billy taught Sparky to shake hands," Jack finally said, his voice rusty, as if he hadn't used it in a while.

"So he's Billy's pet?"

"Sparky's not a pet. He finds rabbits so we can shoot them." Jack's voice turned mocking. "In season of course."

"I wouldn't imagine anything else," she said.

Jack eyed her, as if wondering if she was making a joke. Then he shrugged and turned away, picked up another piece of wood and split it with an expert stroke. He tossed it on the chopped pile and methodically scooped up another stick.

Nikki sighed. She couldn't make him talk; she had to make him want to help.

"So, may I shake Sparky's paw," she said, "and give him a piece of biscuit?"

"If you insist," Jack muttered. "But Sparky's a pain. And don't let Gran see. She gets upset when we waste food."

Nikki turned so she blocked the view from the kitchen. Stooping, she shook hands with the little dog then slipped him a piece of buttery biscuit. The food disappeared in seconds. Sparky licked his lips and waved his paw again. He had an adorable brown patch over his left eye and a white tail that whipped back and forth, and she sensed Jack liked the dog far more than he pretended. She'd also noticed how Jack had eyed the biscuits, almost as interested as the dog.

"Looks like Sparky wants more," Nikki said, keeping a straight face. "Should I give him the rest?"

"No!" Jack slammed the axe into the chopping block so hard the wooden handle quivered. "People food spoils dogs. I'll eat them."

Nikki passed him the bundle of biscuits. He didn't look too happy about approaching her, but at least he hadn't escaped into the woodshed. And she was even more relieved that he'd put down the axe. "My name is Nikki Drake. I'm a private investigator. Your grandmother hired me to look for your brother."

"You charge us money to stand around and eat biscuits?" Jack asked, his voice sullen.

"There won't be much of a charge," Nikki said. At least he was talking.

"Then what's in it for you? Social Services paying you to come out here and dig up dirt?"

"I just want to find Billy. We know he got off the bus about a mile from here, around nine-thirty last Saturday night. We don't know where he went after that. Your grandmother said he wouldn't hitchhike. What do you think?"

She smiled, desperate to keep Jack talking. But he wouldn't look at her. He silently chewed the biscuits, his gaze locked on the stack of wood.

"Maybe there's a shortcut he took?" she went on, pulling out the map. "I don't know this area like you. So your opinion is important."

That didn't sway him. He just swallowed and wiped his mouth, obviously in a hurry to eat and return to his wood chopping.

"Your grandmother is hoping you can help," Nikki said. "Because this map is hard to read."

She kept her focus on the map, feeling Jack's reluctance even as he edged closer. He jabbed a thumb at the paper then stepped back as if burned.

"Billy would have taken that road," he mumbled. "Not the back trail. This road is the fastest. It's longer as a crow flies, but there aren't as many hills."

Despite Jack's hostility, he was clearly a swift thinker. It hadn't taken him long to figure out their current location and the map scale.

"Okay, great," she said. "And if a car came by, would he have stuck out his thumb?"

Jack set his jaw, looking every bit as stubborn as his grandmother.

"This has nothing to do with curfew or probation or Social Services," Nikki said. "Or bending a few rules. I just want to bring Billy home."

Jack's eyes narrowed on her field pack. "Who exactly do you work for?"

"Myself," Nikki said. "And my client. Who in this case is your grandmother."

"You're not obliged to pass information to the police?"

"Only on a case-by-case basis. And only with approval from my client or the client's attorney. Otherwise, my license could be yanked."

Jack shook some crumbs off the napkin, crumpled it up and jammed it in his pocket. His gaze remained on her the entire time, as if doubting the truth of her words. "I suppose it's like a lawyer," he finally said, more to himself than her. "Do you carry a gun?"

"I'm licensed to carry a weapon, yes."

"Licensed in how many states?"

"Just one, California."

"So you're small time," he sneered. "Exactly how many missing persons have you found?"

"One," Nikki said, her voice thickening. These were the questions Jack's grandmother had the right to ask but hadn't. She crossed her arms. Didn't want to talk about her sister.

Something flickered in Jack's eyes and she could have sworn she caught a hint of compassion. But when he spoke his voice was granite hard. "Gran told me a little bit. She thinks you're a hotshot investigator. And I don't want her disappointed."

"I can't promise results," Nikki said. "But I can promise I won't give up."

He eyed her for a long time, his gaze assessing. Then he gave a grudging nod. "Guess that's all we can expect," he said. "And yes, Billy would have accepted a ride. Maybe he wouldn't have hitched because he always followed Gran's rules. But if someone stopped and offered, he wasn't an idiot. He would have got in."

Jack bent and stroked Sparky's head, outwardly nonchalant but Nikki caught the tremor in his voice. "Guess that means some perv took him."

"There are other possibilities," she said. "Maybe he met with some friends. Found some drugs or alcohol and couldn't resist. Does he have any camping equipment?"

"No. And he never went to bush parties. He would have come home. Even if it was just to make sure this damn dog was fed." Jack remained bent over Sparky, his restless fingers moving over the dog's ears.

Nikki waited, tamping down her questions, sensing he had more to say. Sparky's tail thumped against the ground but he was the only one who seemed happy.

"I know some guys who race along there," Jack finally added. "Thought they might know something. Even suspected they might have hit him. But we talked and they weren't on the road that night."

"Think they were telling the truth?"

"Maybe not at first," Jack straightened, staring into her eyes. "But they weren't lying when I finished."

His statement lacked bravado, full only of the simple truth. Jack reminded her of a friend she'd hung around with the last time she ran away, when Justin had found her sleeping on a park bench and convinced her to go home and finish school. That guy had been no angel either.

She eyed the scar on Jack's right hand. There was still some healing to do, although maybe the skin was permanently discolored. Clearly he had used his fists often. They were getting along so well, she hated to change the tone. But the difficult questions had to be asked. The reaction might be more important than the answer.

"So you worked your car buddies over a bit," she said. "Did you ever do that to Billy?"

"Hell, no!" Jack recoiled as if she'd smacked him in the face. "He's my little brother."

"You didn't give him any reason to leave? What about your grandmother? Did she ever ask you to discipline him?"

Jack's jaw dropped. "Leave Gran out of this," he said, his voice as chilly as his eyes.

"Just covering all the bases," Nikki said. "At one time you were taken away. I can't get in the youth offender files to see the reason. Maybe something here drove you away..."

"That was my fault. Not Gran's. Never hers." Jack pressed his fists against his chest as if afraid of lashing out. "And you can fuck off now."

Nikki knew she was pushing, searching for his hot button. But his control was admirable. At his age, she'd have been going for the jugular. But he might know more than he was saying. For Billy's sake, she had to dig. So she waited, the taut silence broken only by the clothes flapping on the line and the harsh scolding of a scrub jay.

Jack glowered. His breathing was ragged and a muscle in his jaw pulsed. He didn't seem inclined to run her off. But he wasn't talking either. It was obvious he held his grandmother in high esteem. And he'd seemed genuinely shocked by her suggestion that he might have hurt Billy.

"I'm just doing the job your grandmother hired me to do," Nikki said.

"Yeah, but you're way off base." Jack smacked his fist in his hand, the abrupt sound startling. "Gran loves Billy. He's her favorite, deservedly so. She'd never do anything to harm him. Neither would I. Because, I...I love him too."

He reddened, as if embarrassed by the admission, but his emotion gave credence to his words. Which meant Billy's family hadn't driven him away. And she'd use that information to shape her search.

"If throwing out abuse accusations is how you help," Jack went on, his hands still fisted, "we don't want you. How much did you fleece her for?"

"Your grandmother paid seventy-four dollars and promised a batch of biscuits. After tasting her cooking, I consider this to be paid in full."

Jack's mouth twisted, as close to a smile as she'd probably get.

"All right," he muttered. "So what now? Do you think a car hit him?" The sun revealed a telltale sheen to his eyes, and his voice sounded unnaturally high, reminding her that he was only sixteen. One didn't need to be a trained investigator to see that behind the tough exterior, this guy was hurting.

She looked down at the map, taking a mental snapshot of the roads and giving Jack time to regroup, knowing he would hate for anyone to spot his tears.

"I'm going to retrace the route he took," she said, keeping her head dipped over the map. "Starting at the bus stop. Does he have any friends or places where he might be staying? Anyone your grandmother might not know about? Places I should check first?"

"That's a waste of time. He wouldn't be hanging with friends."

"What about girlfriends? Someone from school?"

"No, you don't get it. He'd never willingly upset Gran like this. It's like he vanished into thin air."

Nikki gave a troubled nod. Jack and Mrs. Tanner presented the same picture. And both were very credible. Smitty's phone call today also underscored that there was no obvious reason why Billy had disappeared. Leaving her very little to work with.

She folded the map in half, then in quarters, hesitant to mention Sonja. A psychic seemed like a desperation move. And the Tanners did not seem like a family who placed much stock in tea readings. Of course, they didn't have to know. She'd reimburse Sonja out of her own pocket. And take her for dinner.

"Could I borrow something of Billy's?" Nikki asked. "His favorite thing. I already checked his room but nothing stood out. I thought you'd know what he cares about most."

"Sparky." Jack spoke without an ounce of hesitation. "That dog means the world to him. Billy pays for all his food and sneaks out the window at night to sit with him and give him treats. Gran would have a fit if she found out he was wasting money on store-bought food."

"Where does he get the money?"

"Collecting bottles from the ditch. People drive through here chucking things at the trees. They think everything out here is a dump." He shrugged. "Which it kind of is."

That explained the dog treats hidden in the fan. But she couldn't load Sparky up in the car and drive him to the city. She didn't think that was the type of personal item Sonja wanted.

"Why are you asking about his favorite thing?" Jack asked. "Are you using a psychic?"

Nikki crossed her arms then lowered them again. Didn't want to look defensive. But Jack was eyeing her with more curiosity than scorn.

"I have an associate who's helped me before," she said. "It might be worth a try."

"Can't psychics talk to animals on the phone?"

"I don't know," Nikki said. "Up until a couple months ago, I never paid much attention to her methods."

"But she helped, right. So check with her. It can't hurt."

Nikki gaped, surprised at Jack's enthusiasm. There was much more to this kid than she'd anticipated, and she was glad he wasn't stuck in juvie. He seemed to be doing well at his grandmother's. He certainly kept the woodpile stocked.

She reached for her phone.

"Your cell won't work here," Jack said. "A lot of this area is a dead zone."

"Then let's go inside and use your land phone."

"Sparky isn't allowed in the house. Gran doesn't hold with pets. We only have him because he was dumped close by and Billy begged to keep him. She agreed, seeing as Billy is her favorite and all." Jack's rueful smile emphasized how open he could be.

"We'll have to drive up to Lena's store," he added.

"There's no 'we'. I work alone."

"But you can't take Sparky without me. He doesn't know you. And he's not used to cars. He'd freak out and bite."

Nikki glanced down at the dog stretched out at the end of his rusted chain, head on his paws, eyes mournful. He didn't look inclined to bite anything, other than a forbidden piece of biscuit. On the other hand, Gunner wouldn't appreciate being stuffed into a stranger's car either. And he definitely would bite if he thought someone was taking him away.

"Will your grandmother mind if you and Sparky go with me for a bit?'

"Not at all." And now Jack's smile was full wattage and almost teasing. "But don't mention the psychic. That's weird."

CHAPTER FIFTEEN

Smitty wiped his brow, hot and sticky after trudging up Ray's rough driveway. No wonder the man kept his gate locked. The ruts would tear the undersides off most vehicles. Smitty had known Ray Gibson for more than ten years but couldn't remember the last time he'd visited. The farm definitely required maintenance.

He should probably offer to help. Ray spent too much time on the road, driving long distances to pick up carcasses and assist with rescues. It was a tough job for a dedicated animal lover. Ray also recorded every detail of the animal's background, working tirelessly with the SPCA and other groups.

At least he had.

For some reason the SPCA had severed their connection. Something about Ray being too zealous. Smitty shook his head. Didn't matter. Ray was eccentric but his kindness to animals was unquestionable, and that made the man okay in Smitty's book.

He crested the hill, glancing around with a knowledgeable eye. Ray's property was approximately ten acres. It had been cleared decades ago, but now shrubs and underbrush had crept back. A massive evergreen stood watch over the two-story farmhouse but it didn't hide the algae that matted the roof. Numerous paddocks and outbuildings separated the house from the barn but all the fencing tilted precariously. Ray was nowhere in sight.

A spotted llama poked its head over a rotting plank. Smitty had always liked llamas but couldn't remember hearing about this particular one. Clearly she had escaped a tough life. An empty eye socket gaped from the right side of her head and one of her ears was ripped and misshaped, leaving a thin strip rather than a typical triangle.

The llama didn't spit and seemed cautiously curious rather than fearful. Smitty walked over and scratched her fuzzy neck, edging to the side so he could avoid staring at the gaping hole. He'd dealt with many injured animals before but the empty socket made him queasy.

"You're lucky you ended up here, sweetie," he murmured. Ray had a gift for restoring animals' trust and his knowledgeable care had brought many rescues back to full health. The man cared as much for animals as he did for people. Maybe more.

Smitty gave the llama one last pat then turned away and continued looking for Ray. The man didn't have many friends and never spoke of family. He preferred to surround himself with animals, content to be reclusive. But animals couldn't help Ray maintain his property.

He'd organize a work detail, Smitty decided, as he passed a donkey paddock with a rail hanging so low it barely reached the animal's knees. He stopped and straightened the plank, tying it to a fencepost with a piece of baler twine, guessing that the donkey remained inside purely out of politeness.

He glanced around, still not spotting Ray. A beat-up truck was parked close to the verandah of the house so Smitty veered toward the left, relieved he'd be able to catch Ray before he left on his rounds.

The wind picked up, a cooling breeze that carried the hint of hay and manure along with a whiff of smoke. A grayish black plume rose from a burning barrel close to the verandah. He walked toward it, almost stepping on a lone blue running shoe. The air wasn't as pleasant here, laced with the smell of burning clothes and plastic. He'd responded to so many car accidents that the distinctive smell left him shuddering.

He glanced inside the barrel. Ray must have been cleaning out his closet. Rags still smoldered and the missing running shoe explained the smell of rubber. It was odd that Ray didn't consider the environment and all the recycling options. The shoe looked in decent shape. Someone might have used them.

He scooped it up, surprised at its small size. Ray had huge hands and feet. Yet this shoe was only a size nine. He felt a vague unease and glanced over his shoulder, but no one was watching.

He gently set the shoe on the ground and strode toward the verandah, relieved the house was upwind. The smells left him uneasy, prompting images he wanted to forget. The single shoe was especially haunting. He hated seeing those on the highway, knowing what they meant. Fortunately, working with the mounted unit insulated him from responding to traffic carnage. And for that he was grateful.

He climbed the farmhouse steps. The porch creaked beneath his weight and a score of cats scattered. He shuffled sideways, avoiding a three-legged tabby and nearly tripping over a bowl filled with freshly chopped liver.

"Hey, Ray," he called, stepping around the bowl and peering through the screen. Damn, more cats. At least five were curled on the tops of two plastic crates. He glanced over his shoulder, suddenly uneasy. Ray rescued all sorts of animals, dogs included. Would a protective Rottweiler suddenly charge around the house?

But no. Ray didn't keep dogs on his property for long. He wouldn't tolerate any animal that couldn't live in harmony with others. He'd been devastated when a rescued terrier had killed one of his cats.

Smitty pulled out his cell and pressed Ray's number again. A phone chimed from inside the house. Six rings, then Ray's polite voice sounded, requesting that the caller leave a message including the carcass location.

Smitty sighed and pocketed his phone. Ray's truck was still here. He must be working in the old horse barn.

He veered to the left, circling the house and passing a chicken coop filled with plump chickens. They squawked in alarm, as if surprised by his presence.

He followed the beaten path to a faded red barn. Five spacious pens were attached to the east side where pigs could run in and out at will. A low trough was filled with water, and fresh straw brightened a corner. Three pigs cooled off in a concrete section, escaping the flies by wallowing in a manmade waterhole. They looked big and fat and happy, their bellies swollen with contentment.

Closer to the barn, two spotted sows nosed the ground, bickering over the head of a broken mop. The mop flopped back and forth, reddened and matted. One of the pigs grabbed it then flipped it aggressively with her snout.

A face stared up at Smitty—a distorted human face. The eyes and nose were gone but the teeth remained, along with crushed bone and shiny white cartilage.

"Oh, Jesus!" He jerked back so quickly he stumbled. His stomach lurched and he dropped to his knees. Planted his palms on the ground and retched. The entire contents of his gut came up, but still he choked and gagged and heaved, struggling to accept the sight. And what it meant.

Something moved. He twisted, his hands still splayed over the ground. His eyes widened and he raised his arm, desperate to ward off the blow. But he was too late. And the steel shovel was only a blur of movement before it cracked into the side of his head.

CHAPTER SIXTEEN

Nikki followed Jack's directions, turning her car west and then east on the curving blacktop. "How far away is Lena's store?" she asked.

"Two more miles," Jack said, his gaze pinned on the ditch.

"You're sure this is the quickest way?"

"Yup."

Nikki eased the car around a deep rut. Jack had coaxed her into letting him ride along, claiming that Sparky needed him and also that he could direct her to a spot with cell phone coverage. But she had an excellent memory; the map was still vivid in her brain. And the directions Jack was giving weren't the quickest but more likely the route he thought his brother had taken. Not surprising. She would have done the same thing in his situation. Would have wanted to check every road in the county.

But what if Billy's body was lying in the ditch? Bloody and battered. Ripped apart by wildlife. Jack shouldn't see that. On the other hand—and she didn't want to voice this fear—it seemed more likely Billy had been abducted. If so, seven days was far too long to expect a happy outcome.

She glanced in the rearview window, checking on Sparky. The dog may not have been on many car rides but he was certainly taking this one with aplomb. He'd squeezed in beside the cardboard boxes from the Doberman kennel and had his nose pressed against the side window, studying the ditches with the same intent expression as Jack.

"Better open Sparky's window a crack," Jack said. "He's nuts about Billy and has a great nose. If he gets within a half mile, he'll find him."

"So we're actually retracing all his possible routes? Not driving directly to the store?"

Jack shifted on the seat. "Yeah," he admitted. "I have my license but we don't have a car. This is my only chance to check some of the other roads."

"Okay," she said, appreciating his honesty. "But let's do it properly."

She lowered the windows, easing so close to the ditch that her tires crunched over the gravel. "We'll check this side first, then drive back and do the other side. But if we see something, you don't get out. Agreed?"

Jack glanced at her, his mouth twisted. But he didn't answer. Didn't agree to anything.

"I'll turn around, take you back," she said, holding his gaze. "Unless you promise."

"No you won't. And I don't want to make a promise I can't keep."

"How do you know I won't take you home?"

"Because I can help," Jack said. "And it's obvious you're really determined to find Billy."

Her mouth tightened and she stared over the wheel, surprised he could read her so well. But he needed to follow directions if he were to ride along. She'd seen bodies before. It was agonizing, even more gut wrenching when it was someone you love. No way was she exposing him to that.

She looked back at him, hardening her gaze, copying Justin's flat stare, the one that always had people jump to do his bidding. But Jack only lifted a mocking eyebrow. Clearly he'd squared off with far more intimidating people. Still, she couldn't let him ride along, even if his knowledge of the area would be helpful.

She flashed her indicator light and began a U-turn.

"Wait!" Jack said, suddenly animated "I promise that I won't freak out. And I've seen some shitty things. And I can promise not to get in your way. Let me stay...please."

He made it sound like it was her decision and the "please" was a nice touch. She didn't know what he intended to do in his future but he already seemed to have a good understanding of psychology.

"All right," she said, straightening the car. "But I also want you to show me where Billy's school is. Even though you don't think it's relevant."

"No problem," Jack said quickly. "I can take you to the principal's house too."

"You know where he lives? You've been there?"

"Sure, back when I was twelve. On Halloween."

"I don't imagine you were trick or treating," she said.

Jack just winked and turned his attention back to the ditch. Sparky did too, jamming his head out the window, his nose snuffling.

Hiding her smile, she resumed her turtle speed along the shoulder of the road, surprised to admit she appreciated both Jack and Sparky's company. They didn't replace Gunner, but they were decent company in a wooded area that was both unfamiliar and isolated. And if Billy was as smart and intuitive as his older brother, he was a real crackerjack.

She just prayed she'd have the pleasure of meeting him.

CHAPTER SEVENTEEN

"This place belongs to Billy's principal?" Nikki eased her car to a stop, appraising the house. It looked far more prosperous than the other two homes she'd visited today. And much newer. Oversized glass windows extended around the front of the house, shaded by deep overhanging eaves. The tile roof was spotless, and the stone and wood exterior gave a rustic feel. The front lawn was landscaped and someone had been using precious water with abandon. No other way the ornamental shrubs would be so lush.

"Yeah," Jack said. "David Dunbar. He's a real douche. Inherited some money and wants everyone to know how special he is."

"Single?"

"Of course." Jack scoffed. "No grown woman would put up with him. If you're interested, you're not as cool as I thought."

"Just figuring out if he's home," Nikki said. A lone vehicle was parked in the circular driveway, a late-model Ford Bronco. Not a speck of dust marred its metallic red coat, remarkable for anyone driving on these roads. A vanity plate read: YesUCan.

"He's home," Jack said, inclining his seat and propping his dirty boots on the dash. "I'll wait here."

"Yes, you will." She shoved his feet back on the floor, ignoring his half-hearted protest. Jack had turned rather surly after their unsuccessful check of the ditches. In her opinion, not finding any evidence that Billy had been hit by a car was a good thing. Jack, however, seemed to consider their search a failure.

She peered over her shoulder at Sparky. The dog's mood was unaffected. He seemed delighted to drive around in an air-conditioned car, rather than remain home chained to his kennel. At some point he'd curled up in a ball, no longer interested in sticking his head out the window and helping. Gunner never would have quit that quickly. In fairness, Sparky was probably more of a ground sniffer than an air scent dog. But dammit, she missed her dog.

She pushed open her car door, still eyeing Sparky. "We should have grabbed a piece of Billy's clothing from your closet. All that driving around, Sparky might not have even known we were looking for him."

Jack grunted. "He knows. Sparky doesn't need fancy training to remember what Billy smells like. He can find rabbits and partridge quick enough. Don't dis him because he's a mutt who didn't attend K9 finishing school."

"That's not what I was doing," she said. But in a way it was. Gunner had been bred for police work and had received extensive training before he rebelled and Justin gave him to her. Whether it was an animal or person, when she showed Gunner a scent he remained focused. He certainly wouldn't have curled up in the back and taken a nap. In fact, he would have behaved more like Jack, worried and despondent because he hadn't succeeded in finding anything.

"Anyway, this visit is a waste of time so hurry it up," Jack said, tapping impatiently on the dash. "Dunbar couldn't find his way out of a wet paper bag. It's more important to get to the store so we can call your psychic."

"I'll take as long as I need," Nikki said, reaching in and removing the key. It was unlikely Jack would take off with her car but considering his impatience, it was better to be safe than sorry. Though he was probably quite capable of hotwiring her Subaru in seconds. From the looks of his hands, he'd been burned before. But she wasn't going to make it easy.

If Jack was bothered by her lack of trust, he didn't show it. He eyed the house, his fingers still tapping an edgy dance. "If Dunbar gets too creepy, give me a holler. I'd be more than happy to help."

"Thanks, but I can handle a school principal."

Jack gave a glimmer of a smile. "No doubt. But that man's wee brain quits working when he has a hard-on. Thinks he's God's gift. And when a woman who looks like you lands on his doorstep, he's going to think he died and went to heaven. Or that you're trying to pick him up."

Nikki rolled her eyes, scooped up her pack and slammed the driver's door. Jack was still talking but she didn't want to hear any more about Dunbar. Wanted to form her own opinion. Clearly Jack resented authority and was very biased.

A smiling man whipped open the front door before she was even halfway up the flagstone walk.

If this was David Dunbar, he wasn't a bad looking guy. Actually quite handsome in a preppy sort of way. She hadn't known what to expect from the way Jack spoke. The man had sun-streaked hair and was rather nattily dressed for a Saturday afternoon at home:

crisp beige chinos and a white polo shirt. He probably spent a lot of money on his haircuts. Not her type but someone who shouldn't be distasteful to interview.

"Lost?" he asked with a charming grin. "Or do you have car trouble?"

"Neither," Nikki said, pulling out her ID. "I'm a private investigator. If you're David Dunbar I just want to ask some questions about Billy Tanner."

He barely glanced at her ID before swinging the door welcoming wide and ushering her in. "Come inside. You might as well sit down and be comfortable. And please call me Dave."

She stepped through the doorway. It was just as attractive inside, a modern open-air concept boasting vaulted ceilings and exposed beams. His kitchen gleamed with high-end appliances and the sitting area was tastefully furnished, full of black and chrome tables and crafted leather furniture with reverse seams.

"Would you like some coffee?" he asked, his smile turning a little smug as he caught her appraising gaze. "Perhaps a glass of wine? I had a new cooling room installed and would love to put it to use."

"No thank you. I just have some quick questions."

"Please, have a seat." Dunbar gestured at a leather sectional with a reclining footrest. "Although I'm not sure how much I can help. I gather Billy is in some sort of trouble?"

She gave a little murmur, reluctant to reveal too many details. Although she figured she wouldn't have to say much. Clearly Dunbar liked to talk, probably a result of his occupation. Or maybe he was lonely on the weekends. Either way, he was the flirty type who wouldn't be silent for long. She bypassed the sofa, choosing to keep her distance and sit in a nearby chair, accepting that she'd been affected by Jack's opinion.

"Billy's missing," she said. "That's all we know."

"Actually Billy's grandmother called me on Monday," Dunbar said. "Worried that he hadn't come home. I pulled his file and had a look. There's not much in it, certainly not like his older brother. Now *that* one was a handful. Terrible influence on other students, bad to the core. Not surprising he ended up in juvie. I imagine he's still there?"

"I'm here to talk about Billy," Nikki said, annoyed by the man's smug satisfaction, even more alarming for someone who was supposed to care about youth education.

"Of course." Dunbar gave an agreeable nod. "Like I said, Billy's file is unremarkable. Not much to him. He hasn't been in school all week. But he's the type that will drop out and that's certainly something I predicted."

"Did he seem worried, withdrawn? Did his teachers notice anything?"

"Not a thing. He was always quiet. Barely noticeable."

"What about his friends? Do they know anything?"

"No, and we'd have heard if they did. It's a small school and I'm aware of everything that happens. I'm at the school until five, supervising all the afterschool programs. My days are extremely long."

"Indeed," Nikki said, wondering what he'd think of Justin's hours.

"Yes," Dunbar went on. "I believe in an open door policy. Students appreciate it. I like to be a role model. Many of them drop by after school just to chat."

"Did Billy do that?"

"What?"

"Stop by and chat?"

Dunbar gave a dismissive shake of his head. "Like I said, he's not the type. He always jumped on the school bus as soon as the bell rang. Wasn't involved with any extracurricular events. That type of family lacks motivation."

Nikki felt herself bristle. "Billy might enjoy some of the activities if he didn't have a bus to catch. Do you provide transportation for the students who stay after hours?"

"No, we don't have a budget for that. But parents are happy to pick up their kids. It's never an issue."

"Unless a parent, or grandmother, doesn't have a car," Nikki said. She shifted, pressing further back against the soft leather, needing a moment to control the bite in her voice. But this was a vicious circle.

Her mother had faced similar challenges, trying to drive Nikki and her sister to activities, all the while struggling to earn a paycheck. And the less that kids participated, the less they stayed involved. She'd been lucky they lived in the city and could often find a public bus. But Jack and Billy lived in the country, so isolated they even lacked internet. And someone as prideful as Mrs. Tanner would never want her grandsons to accept rides from strangers, well-intentioned or not.

Dunbar flashed a brilliant white smile, so perfect Nikki suspected he'd practiced it in a mirror. "Naturally if a student's parents are busy, I'm happy to let them wait in the clubhouse."

"How kind."

Dunbar preened, oblivious to her sarcasm. "Yes. I love my job and the students seem to appreciate my involvement. Although it is refreshing to spend time with an adult. Are you sure you don't want any wine?"

His voice thickened, his gaze dropping so that he seemed to be speaking to her chest. "I have the entire afternoon free," he said.

She straightened, realizing that when she leaned back, her shirt had tightened over her breasts. And Dunbar had taken it as an invitation. He wasn't only a douche bag but an idiot and a lecher. She couldn't imagine parents wanting their daughters to be alone with this man.

"I'm leaving now." She rose and flipped a business card onto the table. "If you hear anything about Billy, please call."

"Of course. But I'm sure there's no need to worry. And if you're out this way some other weekend, drop by. I'd be happy to see you." He spoke as if he were extending her a remarkable invitation.

"Thank you, but my boyfriend and I are usually busy at the shooting range."

Disappointment flashed across Dunbar's face but he rallied quickly. "Well, if you like sports, our volleyball and soccer teams are both headed to the finals. And our science fair is next month."

Nikki was already heading toward the door, but she paused. Then turned around. "I was talking to someone earlier about their science project. Does Katarina Shebib go to your school?"

"Yes."

His answer was surprisingly brief for a man so eager to impress, and Nikki lingered by the door, watching his expression. "It sounded like she's working on an interesting project," Nikki said. "Pigs cleaning up yards. No mess, no fuss and little expense."

"Yes, indeed. I helped her quite a bit with that." Dunbar puffed out his chest, loquacious once again. "In fact, I was the one who gave her the idea. I also suggested she enter it in the 4-H contest. She's the type of student who could take top prize."

"Is she also the type of student who stayed after school?"

"Yes, of course."

"The type who visited you after hours?"

"Yes." Dunbar's voice was clipped now.

"Does she have a boyfriend? Another student at the school?"

"She did, but they're no longer dating." He crossed his arms but that movement couldn't hide the flush climbing his neck. "And that's not really your business."

"We'll see," Nikki said, stepping outside.

She hurried to her car, practically huffing as she sucked in mouthfuls of clean air.

Jack leaned over and pushed open the driver's door. "Yeah," he said. "Dunbar has that effect."

He straightened, jabbing his hand in a one-finger salute at the man watching from the doorway.

Nikki slid behind the steering wheel, noting her open dash and the binoculars lying on Jack's lap.

"I was just keeping an eye out," Jack explained, replacing the binoculars and clicking the dashboard shut. "Great glasses by the way. But I couldn't find your gun. I was hoping Dunbar would annoy you enough that you'd shoot him. You do have a gun, right?"

"It's rude to snoop in someone else's car." She spoke with a total lack of heat though, rather moved that Jack had been prepared to come to her rescue. "How well do you know that man?"

"Not well. He likes girls not boys."

"I can picture him befriending insecure girls."

"Yeah, they're easy pickings. Especially ones who've been dumped by their boyfriends. That's the way he rolled when I was in school."

"Do you know a girl called Katarina Shebib? Father owns a Doberman kennel?"

"Vaguely. But she's closer to Billy's age. I know they often talked about dogs and she's big into 4-H. Billy mentioned she was one of Dunbar's science groupies."

Nikki drove around the circular driveway, her thoughts whirling. In her message to Justin, she'd alluded that the judge might have been sexually involved with Katarina. But Dunbar seemed a more likely candidate. At least it meant that Tyson Shebib had less motive to kill the judge. For that, she was relieved.

"Did you know Katarina is pregnant?" she asked.

Jack grunted. "Not surprised. Dunbar is too special to use a rubber."

She eased the car to a stop at the end of the driveway and turned her full attention on Jack. "So Dunbar could be the father?"

"Absolutely. But why the interest?"

"Just making conversation," she said.

Jack gave her a cynical look, as if guessing there was more to it. But he didn't speak anymore about Dunbar, just jabbed his thumb to the left, directing her along a twisty gravel road heading west.

"Lena's store is on a hill," he said. "About a mile away. Cell phones work there. Let's hope your psychic knows what she's doing. I've never heard one talk to a dog before."

"Don't get your hopes up. Sonja might not even agree to it."

"Let's hope she does," Jack said, his voice accusing. "Because it looks like you're fresh out of leads."

CHAPTER EIGHTEEN

Five minutes later, Nikki pulled into the parking lot of a low wooden building with a broken Coke sign flashing in the window. Two gas pumps sat close to the door and a faded white awning protected a row of assorted fruits and vegetables. Lena's General Store, a sign proclaimed.

"We always park to the right," Jack said, gesturing out his side window. "Good reception there and Lena won't see us."

"She doesn't let you park here?' Nikki asked, swerving to the side of the gravel lot, out of sight of the watchful proprietor.

"Not if we don't buy anything. Guess she thinks we'll steal all her fruit. It's organically grown," he added, rolling his eyes.

"I'll go in afterwards and buy some coffee. Show her Billy's picture. Find out if she saw him last Saturday."

"Waste of time. The store is too far from the bus stop. Billy wouldn't have walked back here."

"Judging by the map, it's only a half mile from the bus stop," she said. "And I want to cross it off. That's what investigative work is all about."

"Boring shit."

"Most of it is," she said. "Is this store open past eight?"

"Yes, until ten on Saturday nights. But like I said, there's no reason for Billy to come here. He doesn't smoke or drink. And Lena's coffee sucks."

Nikki didn't argue. Jack's negative bouts were draining. Hopefully she hadn't been like that when she was looking for her sister, but guilt could drag anyone down. Although Jack didn't have anything to be guilty about.

She scooped up her phone and checked the service. Two bars were displayed. Not much but enough to reach Sonja. There was also a message from Justin. She'd call him first, before he wasted time digging into Katarina Shebib.

"Please step out of the car for a minute," she said.

"No way. I'm staying right here." Jack's eyes glinted with dark humor. "Sparky is underage. A family member needs to be present during questioning."

"I'm not calling the physic yet. This is another matter. A different case."

"All right." Jack blew out a grievous sigh. "But you shouldn't be working another case on Gran's dime. Not cool."

Grumbling, he stepped from the car and propped a hip on the front bumper. Out of the car but definitely not out of earshot.

She glanced in the rearview mirror. "What do you think, Sparky?" she asked, talking to him the way she would to Gunner. "How about we move that stubborn guy off the car? You okay with that?"

The dog's eyes opened a crack. His tail thumped. He didn't appear worried about Jack, only happy his nap wasn't coming to an end. It was hard to picture Sparky rousing enough energy to chase a rabbit. Probably Jack and Billy pretended the dog was a good hunter so that their grandmother allowed him to stay.

She slipped the gear into reverse and eased backwards. Jack stumbled, then lost his balance and slid to the side of the car. He straightened, shaking his head in mock incredulity. Then he brushed the dust off his jeans, gave his patented shrug and sauntered further away.

Nikki grinned. Was still smiling when Justin answered her call.

"Any luck finding your boy?" Justin asked. "How did the family check out?"

"Fine. Everything appears normal. I'm following up with a couple loose ends but it seems more and more likely Billy didn't choose to leave. The police need to get rolling on this."

"Send me a copy of your report," he said. "I'll make a call."

"Thanks," she said gratefully, knowing Justin would make sure that authorities turned their extensive resources on finding Billy. "I have to get permission from my client before I release the information but I don't expect a problem. She's been pleading for more police involvement the entire week."

Nikki didn't mean to sound accusatory but perhaps her voice had sharpened a bit. Clearly Justin took her comment as criticism.

"Often," he said, "it makes a difference how you talk to the police."

Nikki grimaced, not sure if he was referring to her or Mrs. Tanner. "Sgt. Smith called me today. He seems more concerned. Ready to believe Mrs. Tanner is rightfully worried."

"It's good you stirred things up," Justin said. "And thanks for the tip with the judge. We're taking a deeper look at Tyson Shebib because of your visit."

"About that," she said, "I don't believe Katarina's pregnancy is related to your missing judge. Not anymore. Not after talking to Billy's brother and her principal."

"Sounds like a story there." She felt rather than heard Justin's smile. "Who's putting the disgust in your voice?" he added. "The brother or the principal?"

"The principal. He's a total creep."

"Where are you?" Justin's voice sharpened. "Remember, you don't have Gunner."

"No problem. It's peaceful out here. Nothing but crickets. And I do have backup. Billy's brother is riding with me, along with their dog." Her gaze swept over Jack who stood twenty feet away. He hadn't found anything to lean against but he'd definitely perfected the street corner slouch.

"Perfect," Justin said dryly. "The punk teen. At least you have a dog to keep the creeps away. What kind? Pit bull?"

"Beagle."

His quick chuckle warmed her. That was another great thing about Justin. He kept her relaxed and smiling. And she always felt as if she had backup, having him at the end of her phone. She could run cases by him, knowing his analytic mind would give a different insight. Considering she had access to Sonja's thinking too, she had the far left side covered as well.

"I gotta go, Nik," Justin said. "I hope you can dig up something that will find the kid. Glad his family checked out and isn't involved."

The line went dead. Nikki palmed the phone for another moment, absorbing his words, her troubled gaze on Jack. She was quite confident he had nothing to do with his brother's disappearance. But he was holding something back. The more time she spent with him, the better she was at reading his tells.

She gestured, giving him permission to return to the car. He sauntered back, too cool to rush but his eagerness was obvious in the way he yanked open the door.

"Finally," he muttered. "Now let's hear what your psychic has to say. But first I better let Sparky out for a piss so he won't be distracted on the phone."

Nikki nodded, surprised Jack was more optimistic about the psychic consult than she was. She didn't even know if Sonja could talk to Sparky. Her friend's business revolved around people. Sonja certainly didn't have pet communication listed on her website.

On the other hand, Sonja had once told her that Gunner wanted special dog biscuits. She'd also insisted that he wanted a pony. Nikki hadn't doubted that—Gunner loved being around horses—but that probably could be said about a lot of dogs. At least, it had given Nikki another reason to rescue Stormy, the aged pony who had taught her to ride, and who was now living in comfort at Sonja's farm.

Jack leashed Sparky, opened the hatchback and let the dog jump to the ground. Sparky pulled at the leash, seemingly excited about heading to the coyote brush closer to the building. But Jack growled a command and Nikki heard a flood of liquid as Sparky relieved himself on her back tire.

"You can take him for a little walk," Nikki said. "He probably wants to stretch his legs after being cooped up in the car. I'm surprised he hasn't complained yet."

"The dog is fine," Jack said. He loaded Sparky into the car, settled back into the passenger seat and shot Nikki a sardonic look. "Sparky doesn't complain. He's an animal. Of course, I'm not a psychic so maybe I'm missing something."

"You don't have to be psychic to understand your dog," Nikki reached back between the seats and patted Sparky's velvety head. "A little thoughtfulness goes a long way."

"Gran and I don't hold with spoiling animals," Jack said. "He's lucky she hasn't told Billy to get rid of him."

Sparky poked his head over the console and dragged a pink tongue across Jack's cheek.

"Guess he is kind of cute." Jack gave a grudging smile. "But he hasn't helped find Billy. So he doesn't deserve anything more than a piss break."

"You and your gran are tough customers," Nikki said, pressing in Sonja's number. "I'm calling the psychic now. Just don't expect too much."

At least Sparky looked more alert after his brief trip outside the car. He was still standing, nose poked between the two seats, staring intently through the windshield.

Nikki held the phone to her ear, waiting for Sonja's voice.

"You've reached Sonja's Psychic and Consultants," the throaty message said. "I'm either with a client or the office is closed. You are important to me so please leave a message."

"Well that sucks," Jack said. "Sexy voice though."

Nikki motioned for him to be quiet while she left a message. "Please call me as soon as you can," Nikki said. "It's important, and I won't have cell service for long."

"So now what?" Jack asked. "She calls you back tomorrow?"

"No, if it's important she always calls quickly."

"But what if she doesn't listen to the message for another hour? We can't waste time sitting here, and your phone won't work if we leave."

"We won't have to wait long," Nikki said. "Sonja will know."

"How?"

Nikki shrugged, shifting in the seat and stretching out her legs. She was a reluctant believer and still struggled to understand the psychic thing. She only knew Sonja always called when Nikki needed her.

"So this is what private investigators do?" Jack's lip curled in scorn. "Sit around all day in their cars? Suckering clients into paying an hourly rate?"

"And expenses too," Nikki added with a teasing grin.

"What a rip-off. How long do we sit here?"

Nikki's phone buzzed, saving her from answering. She shot Jack a triumphant look, then grabbed the phone and filled Sonja in on the pertinent details.

Sonja listened silently. Then she laughed. "So that's the personal item?" she said. "A dog?"

"Sparky is who he cares about most," Nikki said.

"Has he been upset since Billy disappeared?"

"A little. But not now." Nikki peered over the seat, checking that Sparky was still awake. "I can bring you something else of Billy's tonight. In the meantime can you talk to the dog? Maybe he saw Billy take a sleeping bag or food into the woods."

"Animals aren't my specialty," Sonja said. "Sometimes I can communicate with them, but not consistently enough to offer it as a service."

"I'm just asking you to try," Nikki said, putting Sonja on speaker. "No expectations."

"But it's not what I do and even harder over the phone."

"Just try already," Jack snapped. At Nikki's sharp glance, he added, "Please."

Sonja heaved a sigh. "What's the dog's name?" she asked.

"Sparky." Nikki and Jack blurted out at the same time.

"Okay," Sonja said. "Hold the phone up to Sparky, still your minds and stay silent. The next person who talks should be me. Remember that...Jack."

It was quiet in the car. Nikki held the phone between the two seats, close to Sparky's head. She turned away, staring out the side window, afraid if she looked at Jack she'd either laugh or cry. And still her mind? How was that possible when anxiety hummed through her gut?

She wondered what Justin would think of her Hail Mary effort. He liked Sonja but he certainly hadn't added her to his detectives' approved consult list. She'd have to ask him if he ever resorted to psychics. If so, which ones.

And though she tried to keep her mind blank, it kept churning with thoughts and fears and questions. The one that gave her the most hope was that Sonja had known Jack's name. Nikki hadn't revealed his name, except to Justin.

She had no idea how many minutes they were silent. Jack, to his credit, didn't move. Didn't talk. Didn't seem to even breathe. At one point, she even glanced over, checking that he was still in the car.

When they finally heard Sonja speak again, they both whipped around in their seats, staring at the phone and the dog.

"I didn't get much," Sonja said. "Sparky's confused and lonely and misses Billy. Says he hasn't been getting any treats lately. But he really liked the white thing he had today. He wanted more. Way more."

"Must have been the piece of biscuit," Nikki said.

"What crap," Jack muttered. "How is this going to help?"

"Sparky was very open and receptive," Sonja said. "Maybe *you* should be a little more open, Jack."

Jack rolled his eyes.

"Was there anything else?" Nikki asked, privately sharing Jack's disappointment. "Anything about where Billy might be?"

"Take me off speaker please," Sonja said. And all the lightness in her voice had disappeared.

Nikki pressed a button. "You're off," she confirmed, pressing the phone to her left ear, trying to keep it far away from Jack's sharp ears.

"Do you see a big box?" Sonja asked. "Sparky wants you to check it."

"There is something like that here," Nikki said, feeling Jack's gaze sharpen. She kept her eyes straight ahead, didn't want him racing to the dumpster to the left of her car. The metal bin squatted only forty feet away, close to an employee side door, a cavernous steel container big enough to hold a body.

"Thanks, Sonja," she added. "I'll drop by with some of Billy's clothing later."

Nikki cut the connection and looked at Jack. "Can you go inside and grab us something to drink. Get a hotdog too if you're hungry. There's money in the console."

"What did she say?"

"Not much. Sparky doesn't have a big vocabulary so it's only guesswork. You know, like calling a biscuit the white thing."

Jack smacked his fist into the palm of his hand, the noise vibrating through the small car. "Tell me what she said! You don't understand. Billy's my brother!"

Nikki sighed. Earlier she would have been alarmed by Jack's aggressiveness. Now she felt like opening her arms and wrapping him in a comforting hug. She certainly didn't want to open that dumpster with him beside her. Seeing a dead body was hard. When it was a loved one—thrown away like garbage—the pain was crippling. She knew that firsthand.

Jack laced his fingers together then pressed them against his lap, struggling to keep his emotions in check. "Please tell me. I know she said something bad."

Nikki glanced at Sparky. He wagged his tail, delighted with his odd day. Surely he wouldn't look so happy if he thought his beloved owner was stuffed in a garbage bin? A box, Sparky had called it.

"All right," she said slowly. "Sonja wants me to check something."

"What?" Jack asked. "Whatever it is, I'm coming with you."

"Only if you agree to follow in my steps. You know...in case we have to preserve evidence."

"Don't make excuses. I know the ground's too dry for prints. I'm not stupid."

No, he wasn't stupid. And Nikki's heart ached for him, and what they might find. "Let me go first. Just in case. Agreed?"

She waited until he gave a curt nod. Then she reached in her bag and pulled out two pairs of latex gloves.

"This is what Sonja said." She passed him a pair of gloves. "Sparky wants us to check a big box. I believe that means the dumpster behind the store."

Jack's gaze shot to the steel bin. The blood drained from his face. "Oh fuck," he said.

CHAPTER NINETEEN

Nikki and Jack sat for a moment, staring at the metal garbage bin. Then Jack scraped a hand over his bloodless face, pushed open his door and stepped out. He waited by the hood of her car, staring at the ground, slowly tugging on his gloves.

He wasn't in any hurry to look either, Nikki thought, stepping from the car and adjusting her gloves.

They trudged single file toward the bin with Jack walking so close behind her that his ragged breath fanned the back of her neck.

She stopped in front of the squat bin and pulled in a cautious sniff. The air wasn't pleasant but it certainly wasn't repulsive. Nothing that screamed of rotting meat. But plastic could serve as a good scent barrier, especially cling wrap.

Steeling herself, she grabbed the handle and swung back the lid.

Flies rose in a swarm around her face. Pesky brown ones, too small to be blowflies. She clamped her mouth tight, rose on her toes and peered in. Then squeezed her eyes shut in an overwhelming moment of relief. There was nothing in there but a pile of rotting carrots: greenish-orange ones with limp tops. In some places, the bottom of the bin was visible, spotted with clumps of dried lettuce.

Jack squeezed up beside her. She heard his exultant chuckle. Then his choke as he swallowed a fruit fly. He backed away, choking and spitting but still grinning from ear to ear.

"Damn, that Sparky is useless," he said. "Scaring us like that. All he thinks about is food."

Nikki dropped the lid with a clang. They walked back toward the car, side-by-side, their steps much lighter than during their approach.

"Your job sucks," Jack said. "How can you do this every day? My heart was in my throat."

"Most of my work isn't like this. Most of it is boring. Checking insurance claims, process serving or tailing an errant spouse."

"When did you start?"

"I was sixteen when I started part-time work in an investigator's office, learning the ropes. My official apprentice period took about three years. I went out on my own awhile ago."

"At least you don't have to put on a police uniform. And turn into an asshole."

"Police have a tough job. Without them, there'd be anarchy."

"I suppose," Jack said. "Guess I feel a little sorry for them now. Don't even want to think about what they see."

"Let's take a break," Nikki said. "Grab a drink. And I want to show the owner Billy's picture. See if she remembers him."

Jack didn't even argue that it was a waste of time. They climbed the three worn wooden steps, companionably close, and entered Lena's country store. An overhead bell tinkled, announcing their arrival. A woman with a gray ponytail and thick-lensed glasses glanced up from behind a sturdy counter. Her back was bent and stooped, and she appeared to be at least eighty.

"Finally," she said, peering at Jack. "I had carrots put aside. But they're all spoiled now and I had to dump them." Her voice turned accusing. "I thought you were coming back on Saturday, Billy?"

Nikki stepped forward, passing the woman her card. "I'm Nikki Drake. And this isn't Billy. It's his brother. We're looking for Billy. I gather he was here recently. Was it last Saturday night that you expected him?"

The woman nodded, her annoyance turning to concern. Over the next ten minutes she answered all Nikki's questions, speaking slowly and thoughtfully. Apparently Billy stopped by regularly, looking for old or misshapen carrots. He'd told Lena all about Radar and his job at the horse stable. And he'd never missed a pick-up before.

"I see you have a surveillance camera," Nikki said. "May I take a look?"

"I'm sorry, no," Lena said, shooting a wary look at Jack. "That camera outside is fake. A lot of teens park here for hours at a time."

"Not surprising," Jack cut in. "This is the only place with reception in a ten-mile radius."

"Yes, but you people don't have to block the gas pumps and intimidate my customers. Or steal fruit from the bins. Be like your brother and ask first."

Jack scowled. Then gave a slow nod. "Okay," he said. "I'll talk to the boys."

Five minutes later, Nikki and Jack returned to the car with two homemade chocolate chip cookies, compliments of Lena, along with a new understanding of the area where Jack and his friends were welcome to park.

"I'm going to take you home," Nikki said. "And update the police. What we found will energize their search."

"But Billy could be anywhere by now," Jack said, dropping his uneaten cookie into the cup holder of the console. "The interstate is accessible from here. Maybe some pervert gassed up at Lena's, then grabbed him. We have no way of tracking it."

"Police will check store sales for that night," Nikki said.

"And highway cameras. There's a bank machine inside so they can request that information as well. They have access to tons of stuff, much more than I do. This is all helpful."

Though her voice was calm, she gripped the steering wheel with both hands, her palms clammy. Billy had been missing for seven long days, and it was impossible not to imagine the horrors he might be enduring. And the thought of Mrs. Tanner waiting hopefully in her kitchen left Nikki aching.

"This is my fault." Jack rubbed his face in misery. "I wouldn't let him take carrots from our garden. But why did he have to worry so much about damn horse treats?"

"Your brother loves animals. Sgt. Smith said he brought carrots all the time. It's no one's fault. Certainly not yours."

"Gran warned us not to hitchhike," Jack went on. "But I didn't want to stay out here in the sticks. Billy probably thought it was okay to hitch rides too. I never thought anything like this would happen."

"Of course you didn't." Nikki studied his expression, feeling another nudge of suspicion. "There's still a chance he hooked up with that youth gang," she said. "You know...the ones *he* was with when he tossed those fire bombs."

"No," Jack muttered. "He wasn't in a gang. He never liked the city. Not like me. He's the good grandson. The one with no record."

Nikki absorbed the misery etched on Jack's face, the sort of look she'd worn when her sister had gone missing. She also remembered Sonja's statement that Jack should be honest. And Nikki knew now what he was hiding. And why the skin on his right hand was pale and puckered.

"It was you that night, wasn't it?" she said.

Jack shook his head but a muscle twitched in his jaw.

"Social Services would have taken you," she went on. "So Billy claimed he threw that firebomb."

Jack crossed his arms, staring straight ahead.

"If we knew Billy wasn't involved with your old gang," Nikki said, "the police won't waste any more time checking the usual city spots. It could help find him."

It was quiet in the car, silent except for the hum of the engine. And Jack's ragged breathing.

Jack finally broke. "I didn't ask him to take the fall," he muttered. "Billy insisted. Said it would kill Gran if they took me. He made me promise to get my shit together. And I have. But now I lost my brother."

Nikki sighed, already piecing together new scenarios. So Smitty was correct. Billy hadn't been upset when he left the barn that night. He hadn't wanted to ditch his community service either. And he certainly hadn't been looking for any street friends. All he'd wanted was horse carrots.

"All right," she said. "Let's assume he was in a great mood when he stepped off that bus. He wants to pick up the carrots and Lena's store closes at ten. Would he walk there on the road or take a shortcut?"

"He'd stick to the road," Jack said. "There are lots of game trails that he knows from hunting and snaring. But they'd be slow-going in the dark."

"Does he have any friends who live between the bus stop and Lena's store? Any place he might have stopped?"

"No, he wasn't into girls or hanging out. All he did was talk about horses. Especially that one with the nasty burn." Jack paused, his face turning a guilty red.

Nikki gave a reassuring nod. "I saw Radar yesterday. He's doing well."

"I never meant to hurt any horse," Jack said. "We just wanted to get back at the cops for always hassling us. I thought the trailer was empty...until I heard the screams." He slumped back against the seat. "Billy mentioned that the horse liked carrots. They helped keep him quiet when he rubbed on ointment. Guess that explains why Billy was backtracking to the store."

Nikki veered east along a nondescript gravel road, following Jack's instructions for the quickest way home. She didn't want to think of poor Radar. She just wanted to drop off Jack so she could talk candidly on the phone.

Billy had disappeared somewhere between the bus stop and the store. That information was crucial. If only the police had been told he had nothing to do with the fire bombs, they would have taken Mrs. Tanner more seriously. Still, Nikki empathized with Jack and was even more awed by Billy's courage. And his loyalty. Mrs. Tanner certainly had raised two unique boys.

She whipped around another corner, peppering gravel against the bottom of her car. Fortunately there was no traffic. A black truck sat on the narrow shoulder, but so far it was the only vehicle they'd met.

She glanced idly at the pickup in her rearview mirror: a late model Ford-150. The license plate was coated with dust but the parking decal in the window was familiar.

She braked so sharply Sparky slid forward, his paws scrambling for traction between the two seats.

"What is it?" Jack asked, swinging out his arm and rescuing Sparky.

She didn't answer. Just backed up in front of the deserted pickup, stepped out and peered through the driver's window.

It was definitely Smitty's truck. Empty coffee cups littered the floor and the GPS was mounted in the same spot. There were more cups in the back. The bed was empty of hay but four bales had been stacked on the side of the road, barely five feet from the tailgate and close to a locked gate with a "NO TRESPASSING" sign.

The passenger door clicked as Jack stepped from the car. He sauntered over, glancing at the truck, then the hay. "What's up? Yo, look at that dead deer."

He cupped his hands around his eyes and peered through the tinted window. "No one's hurt. Why'd you stop?"

Nikki pulled out her phone, checking for reception. Nothing, not a single bar. Besides, she couldn't call Smitty and ask why he was parked on the side of the road. Lara said he was a community volunteer. Perhaps he'd hit the deer then pulled over to move the carcass off the road. If that was his practice, it would explain why his truck bed was stained with blood. Still, the fact that he was cruising around Billy's neighborhood, less than twenty-four hours after she'd questioned him, raised all sorts of questions.

Jack walked behind the hay, expertly appraising the deer. "Lot of meat on that doe. Let's tie it on your roof and take it home. Gran will be delighted."

Nikki studied the rutted driveway, her mind whirling. This wasn't even close to Smitty's home. Earlier she'd pinpointed his address in relation to Billy and it definitely wasn't this far east.

"Any idea who lives up there?" she asked.

"No idea," Jack said, tugging at the deer's hind legs. "But we gotta grab this deer. Finders keepers. Got any rope?"

Nikki pivoted, eyeing the chain link fence with the high wings extending into the brush—an expensive gate out of place at the bottom of the narrow driveway. Someone wanted privacy. She couldn't help but wonder why.

"Hey, help me out here," Jack called. "What are you doing?"

Alerted by her silence, he released his hold and the deer's hindquarters thumped back to the ground. "Oh, hell," he said. "You think this pickup has something to do with Billy?"

He sprinted around the truck and dropped to his knees beside the front bumper.

"Come here!" he shouted. "Bring a light. There's brown hair. And blood. Oh, hell."

"It's okay, Jack," she said. "I examined this vehicle last night. The grill wasn't cracked. The driver probably did that today when he hit the deer."

Jack rose from his crouch, relief washing his face. Then his eyes narrowed. "So you were already suspicious of this guy? That means you think he was involved. Or else you wouldn't have stopped."

He raced back, skidding to a stop mere inches in front of her. "Whose truck is it? Tell me. Bet it belongs to one of those asshole cops, the horse police. That's it, isn't it?"

Jack was too smart. And she still wasn't sure what to make of Smitty being parked here. It was probably nothing. Admittedly if Smitty wasn't a cop, her radar would be quivering even more than it was now.

"Tell me," Jack demanded.

"It's probably nothing," she said, repeating the words that were going through her head. "But I'm going to wait by the truck so I can talk to the owner. How far away is your house?"

"Too far to walk," he said, his eyes blazing. "I'm staying with you."

"No, I need to be alone for this. I'm just hanging around to talk to an acquaintance."

"No," Jack said, studying her face. "You have a different expression. Like you're onto something. It's the same look as when you thought I was hurting Billy."

Nikki sighed, regretting her earlier suspicions. No wonder Jack distrusted authority. "I know you didn't have anything to do with your brother's disappearance," she said. "You've been a big help today."

"So, let me stay."

She sighed. "Okay, but only if you don't jump to conclusions. Remember this is probably nothing. And you have to wait in the car when I talk to him."

"No sweat. I'll be as quiet as Sparky."

Nikki glanced back at her car. At least, they'd be able to give Sparky a longer walk and let him stretch his legs. The dog was so placid, it was easy to forget about him.

Only Sparky wasn't so placid now. He was wheeling circles in the back. Then he scrambled onto the driver's seat and poked his head through the lowered window, whining in excitement.

"He smells the deer," Jack said, shaking his head in exasperation. "He's a pain about food."

Sparky jumped up, scratching at the window with his front paws.

"Useless mutt," Jack said. "Sorry he jumped on your seat. I'll tie him in the back where he belongs."

The dog's whining turned to a high-pitched yip. He abruptly squeezed through the opening, landing awkwardly on the gravel. Then he raced toward the deer, half yelping, half barking. Nikki had never heard such strange noises before. Of course, she'd never seen a beagle around a dead deer either.

But Sparky didn't stop at the deer. He leaped over the carcass and charged into the woods, his yips turning into a series of eerie howls.

"Sparky!" Jack hollered.

The dog reappeared on the other side of the gate, nose in the air, tail straight out. Ignoring Jack, he bolted up the gravel drive and vanished around the bend.

Jack shot forward but Nikki grabbed his arm, stopping him from chasing his dog. "Does Sparky usually come when you call?"

"Usually. Unless he's on a scent. But he never barks weird like that. And he didn't even look at the deer. It's gotta to be Billy." Jack's voice rose. "I'm going to climb that fence."

She tightened her grip on his arm. No way was she letting Jack go up that driveway.

"If Billy's up there," Jack said, his mouth set in a mutinous line, "he needs me. Right now."

Nikki silently agreed. If Billy was there, the arrival of a strange dog would surely trigger panic in his abductor. If that happened, Billy's life might hinge on precious minutes. But they needed backup, needed to let the police know their location.

"Here," she said, pulling out her keys. "Take my car. Use your grandmother's land phone and call the police."

"Yeah, right. They might show up...next week."

Nikki froze, absorbing the truth to his words. Mrs. Tanner had a history with the police; so did Jack. Who knew how long it would take authorities to respond.

She unlocked her phone and thrust it at him. "Go home and call Justin Decker. His number is on the screen. Tell him I need help. I'll get Sparky."

Jack started to protest but must have seen something in her expression.

"That's the best way you can help," she said. "Otherwise we both get in the car and find some hill where we can call. But that will take even more time."

She could feel the tension humming through Jack's body. Along with his indecision. But he pulled in a calming breath and she felt his muscles relax. She released her grip on his arm, ran to her car and pulled the Glock from her bag.

"So you do have a gun," Jack said, his eyes following her every move. "I guess you'll be all right alone?"

"Absolutely,"

She gave him a reassuring nod, waiting until he nodded back. Then she turned and charged into the dense brush, following Sparky's route around the locked gate.

It was slower going than she anticipated. The brush was thick, a mixture of woody eucalyptus and junipers that choked out the young deciduous trees. She ducked beneath a rotting oak and almost tripped over the remains of a rock wall. Thorns grabbed at her shirt, slowing her further. This trail might be passable for a tough little dog but it was painful slogging for humans. It almost seemed as if the brush had been deliberately planted in order to discourage potential trespassers.

She caught a glimpse of blue sky, a welcome beacon in the thick bush, and used it to guide her toward the driveway. Something larger than her had bulled through recently, leaving a wider trail to follow. She pulled free from one last clinging bramble and scrambled onto the gravel clearing. It felt like she'd been bushwhacking for a while, yet she was still only a stone's throw from the gate. At least now she was on the other side of the fence.

Jack spotted her and pressed closer to the steel mesh, one hand gripping the wire, the other wrapped around her phone. Even thirty feet away, his concern was obvious.

"Go," she called, jabbing a thumb at her car. "Drive somewhere. Call Justin."

She didn't know if it would be quicker to go to his grandmother's house or back to Lena's. That was his decision. She only wished he'd move faster.

She gave another impatient gesture then wheeled and sprinted up the driveway, following Sparky's trail.

CHAPTER TWENTY

The man whistled while he worked. Earlier he'd been angry about something, leaving the blood-stained chopping block and returning with a thunderous scowl. But now he was back in the barn, relaxed and happy again. Occasionally the buzzing saw stopped, and he stepped out of view, usually to croon to the pigs as he tossed them...food.

Billy gagged. He pressed his hands over his mouth, swallowing back the bile, trying to absorb this fresh horror. But his mind was sluggish, along with his coordination, and he couldn't stop shivering. He bit the side of his hand, hoping the pain would jumpstart his brain.

He shouldn't even be here. This was a mistake. He'd never starve a dog to death, not like the poor man Mr. Psycho was currently cutting up. It had to be about the police horse. But Radar was alive. He had some burns on his back, bad burns, but he was alive.

Understanding dawned and Billy's hands shook so hard they no longer would cover his mouth. His captor was recreating each scene. He'd starved the prisoner who'd been in the adjacent stall but given Billy hay, grain and water. Just like Radar. That meant the man planned to burn him first. Smitty had always warned that hay was flammable.

Oh, God, no! A choked sob escaped. This wasn't fair. Maybe he could talk to the man, explain. But that wouldn't stop anything. No way he'd let Billy go. He'd just find someone else to stick with his syringe and torture in his pig barn. Maybe he'd go after Jack. Then Gran would be left with no one.

Dammit. This wasn't right. He hadn't even done anything.

But after a moment, Billy pulled in a shaky gulp of air. Squared his shoulders. Feeling sorry for himself wouldn't help. He didn't want to be like the broken man in the next stall, now being carved up into pig fodder. He wasn't going to meekly surrender. He certainly didn't want his back burned. How would Psycho Man do it? Toss in a firebomb?

Billy thought for a moment then shuffled to the back of the stall. The first thing he needed to do was get rid of the hay.

He scooped up a handful and jammed the stalks through the wire mesh and into the next stall. It was agonizingly slow but after seven days of being locked up, at least he had a constructive way to spend his time.

Ray Gibson switched off the meat cutter. Human hair gave pigs indigestion so he liked to shave the heads first. However, Smitty's visit had taken some time, and there were still some highway carcasses that needed pickup.

He pushed the wheelbarrow closer to the pens and tossed in the last of the leg bones. "Don't eat so fast," he admonished Betty, his favorite pig. "There's plenty more."

She continued ripping at the bone, not bothering to lift her snout. He was glad she'd nabbed a juicy piece. Lately, Doris, one of the younger females was pushing Betty around, and it hurt to watch their squabbles. Animals and humans needed to get along. They shared this planet and they should be equals.

He watched the pigs eat for a moment, enjoying their contentment. Betty was so close, he could reach over the low fence and scratch her hairy back. When she was little, he used to keep her in the house but the other pigs had turned jealous, and now he'd learned to hide his favoritism.

"I'll bring you more food later," he crooned. "Some tender young meat that's cooked." He still wasn't quite sure of the appropriate punishment for the horse torturer. He'd tried to pump Smitty for more details about the firebomb but as usual the officer refused to talk about his work.

It might have been impossible to even find out the torturer's name if it hadn't been for Ray's internet friends. Everyone agreed the teenager should atone for his sins. They'd practically begged Ray to do something. Sure, they never came out and actually asked, but Ray knew the animal groups depended on him to make things right.

This was the first time Ray had ever disciplined a youth. Tracking down the underagers was frustratingly difficult. But the kid had been more than happy to climb into Ray's truck. It was as if he just *knew* it was time to repent.

Ray frowned and turned away from the slobbering pigs. He needed more tranquilizers. He'd used the last on the boy and probably had the dosage a little high. At the time, he hadn't known the boy's weight. But he didn't want his pigs eating tainted meat.

He was always particular about what he fed his animals. Some drugs could harm the liver, and it was important to be careful about additives.

However Smitty would be drug free. And the boy had been here a full week. The tranquilizer would be well out of his system by now. It was time.

Whistling, he returned to his bench and assembled a glass bottle, a rag and some gasoline. This wouldn't take long. He just wanted the torturer to apologize, to recognize the error of his ways. After that, everyone could move on. He was certain that in the teen's next life, the boy would be much kinder to animals.

He soaked the rag in oil and carefully taped it to the gas-filled bottle. Then he walked to the front of the stall. But he jerked to a stop, so confused he almost dropped the bottle. The hay was gone, the entire two flakes.

Had the boy eaten it? Oh, no. This wasn't good. He shook his head in dismay. Smitty said there was alfalfa in Radar's trailer. It had caught fire and caused much of the horse's terror. The punishment wouldn't work if the torturer didn't share Radar's fear.

The boy glared up at him. Ray didn't appreciate the look in the teen's eyes. He didn't look at all sorry, not like the scores of people who'd been here before. Even the fancy judge had repented. Maybe the boy had been given too much grain. It was high energy, laden with protein. Smitty said they fed it to all the police horses.

"I like animals," the boy said.

"No talking," Ray snapped. He cupped the gas-filled bottle, wondering how this was going to work. He'd never used a firebomb before. What if the bottle bounced off the boy and burned harmlessly on the floor? It might not be possible to exactly duplicate the boy's crime. Ray certainly didn't want his barn to burn down.

The boy was trembling, sweating with fear. Good. He needed to understand how the horse had felt.

But no. His hair was too slick.

Frowning, Ray opened the stall door and checked the water bucket. It was empty. So it wasn't sweat that dotted the torturer's forehead. The boy had soaked his hair. And his clothes too.

Ray's jaw clenched. It would take hours for it to dry. And he needed the skin to sizzle—just like Radar's.

"Take off your shirt," he snapped.

The boy didn't move.

Ray scowled, then turned and hurried back to his work bench. He pushed aside the stained meat cutter. Buzzing flies lifted in protest, their bodies slow and swollen with blood. He bent beneath the bluish cloud, unlocked the lower drawer and gathered his tools.

Stun gun, handcuffs and blowtorch. That should do the trick. The blowtorch would be safer than a firebomb. And the teen was terrified of the stun gun. Ray only wished he'd remembered to pick up fresh batteries.

He paused, then replaced the stun gun, selecting instead his six-foot cattle prod. It had more kick, and he could place it exactly where he wanted. The last time he'd used it was when he'd cut off the dog torturer's ears.

Happy once more, he headed back to punish the teen.

CHAPTER TWENTY-ONE

Billy sagged. His arms ached and his legs refused to coordinate with his brain. But the handcuffs kept his naked body stretched against the wall.

He tried to balance on his toes and take the weight off his wrists. At first he hadn't thought any shock could be worse than a stun gun, but the electric cattle prod had quickly widened his horizons. His back still seared from where Psycho Man had pressed it. And the air reeked of burnt skin.

He groaned, unable to form coherent words. The man had left, temporarily satisfied with the pain he'd inflicted. But the blow torch still sat by the open stall door. That would be next. The final punishment. Billy doubted he could endure more than five seconds of that torch. He'd scream any apology the man wanted, might even admit it hadn't been him who burned Radar.

But he couldn't do that. Couldn't turn that madman onto Jack. Maybe it would be better to repent now. Avoid any more pain. The worst thing was that they wouldn't find his body. Gran and Jack would be forever waiting.

He swallowed another groan, gathering some satisfaction that he'd briefly flustered his captor. The man had looked so confused when he discovered the hay gone and Billy's clothes wet. Of course,

Billy's satisfaction had been short lived. His captor had only returned with the cattle prod. And Billy had quickly removed his clothes.

Billy flattened his face against the wall, keeping his eyes closed. There was really nothing left to do now but wait. And try to be brave.

Something shuffled in the aisle. His captor must have returned. Judging by the sounds, he was dragging something.

Billy cracked open his eyes, reluctant to look.

He winced at the sight. Another captive. This man was big though, well fed and clearly unconscious. He must have been jabbed with a syringe, just like Billy had been last week. But no, his head was bleeding. And the face looked familiar.

Billy stiffened. *Sgt. Smitty?*

Hope flared and he found the strength to balance on his toes. It was definitely Smitty. The cop was big and tough. When he woke up, he'd rescue Billy. And Jack said police were like ants. If you saw one, there had to be others.

But Psycho Man was reaching for his chainsaw. Oh, God. Billy opened his mouth to protest, but the only sound that came out was a fearful squeak. "No talking," the man had said. And he religiously enforced the rules.

Billy gaped, his words stifled with fear. But this was horrible. Psycho Man was going to cut Smitty up while he was still alive. Before he even woke up. Billy couldn't just stand by and watch.

"Don't, please," Billy managed, his voice rusty. "Don't hurt him."

The man's jaw clenched. "You know the rules. No talking. Until it's time to repent."

"But I'm sorry I burned that horse. I want to talk about it. I want to...repent."

The man's head shot up. "Very good," he said, his eyes glittering. "You see, that wasn't so hard."

"Yes, but you have to understand. I love animals and I'll be good to them now, I swear."

"You will be good to them. In the afterlife. And when you come back to this earth, you'll be a better person. The entire world will be a better place."

"But that man loves animals too," Billy said, his voice gaining strength. "He's good to them. And to people too. He shouldn't be here. He doesn't need to repent."

"I know," the man said, almost sadly. "Now be quiet. Or I'll do you first."

"But you can't cut him up," Billy said, spurred by desperation. "Not now. The...drugs in his system will hurt the pigs. That wouldn't be right, you know, to the animals. It would *hurt* them."

The man's brow furrowed. He set down the chainsaw and strode into the stall. "What kind of drugs?"

"Oxycontin and Vicodin," Billy lied, thinking fast. "We both did them at the police station. Not everything was reported after a bust. We kept a whole tack box full of that stuff."

"Oxy." The man stroked his beard. "Probably take a week to get that out of his system. But you'd be okay."

"No, I wouldn't. It takes months. You better research it."

The man glanced at Smitty's inert body then back at Billy, his forehead wrinkling with indecision.

"We had a lot of drugs at the police station," Billy added. "I don't even know all their names. But you really should check first. Ask a vet or something—"

"Stop talking! I'm trying to think."

Outside a hound was baying and they both glanced toward the side door. Billy hadn't heard a dog on the property before. And his brain must be fried from all the shocks. Because the dog that burst through the doorway and rocketed down the aisle looked exactly like Sparky.

The dog shot into the stall, past the man and jumped on Billy.

"Hey, boy," Billy said weakly. And even though Sparky's claws hurt, it was so damn good to see his dog that his eyes misted. His brain couldn't process it though. First Smitty, then Sparky.

He didn't know what it meant but it sure beat dying alone.

The man seemed confused too. "That dog likes you," he said.

Billy swallowed. If he admitted Sparky was his dog, the man would know rescuers were coming. But were they? Maybe for some reason Sparky had been with Smitty—who was now down and out.

"Just let us go," Billy pleaded.

The man shook his head. "No. My work is more important than any individual. He'd try to stop me."

"But we won't. Please. I promise not to tell."

"No, it's your time." The man stepped out into the aisle and picked up the chainsaw. He strode back into Billy's stall, his eyes shining with purpose.

Billy's throat dried in sheer terror. "Not in front of the dog," he squeaked, glancing down at Sparky who'd curled in a ball and now rested his loving head on Billy's foot. "It will give him nightmares."

The man hesitated.

"Put down the chainsaw," a woman behind them snapped. She looked like a woman from Jack's magazines except that she was fully dressed, and her voice was crisp and authoritative. Best of all she held a gun.

Billy choked, so relieved he sagged against the cuffs.

"You okay, Billy?" she asked.

He nodded.

"Put it down," she snapped. "Now."

The man turned, gripping the saw. He stepped back out into the aisle and edged toward her. She didn't want to shoot him. Billy could see it in her eyes.

Just shoot him, he willed. In the knee, in the arm, even the damn chest. Before Psycho Man gets too close. If Billy had the gun, he wouldn't hesitate. He could scarcely breathe, afraid she'd look at him and the man would jump her.

But she backed up and the man moved with her, both of them edging down the aisle in an odd death dance.

Shoot him! At least she wasn't talking, Billy thought. Her eyes were hard as glass, as if she'd been in this position before. Maybe she knew what she was doing. But he didn't like how she was backing away. And Psycho Man was posed to spring. Billy could see the tautness of the man's shoulders. He watched in horror, not wanting to look but too terrified to turn away.

And then Jack charged out from behind the work bench. He stuck his arm out and jammed the six-foot cattle prod into the man's back. The man screeched and fell to his knees, the chainsaw clattering to the floor.

Billy blinked. His brother was here too? That's why the woman had backed up, drawing the man closer to the bench. And Jack was rather impressive. For a guy who preferred cars and city streets to farms and barn animals, he had an excellent knack for using a stock prod. He gripped the instrument in both hands, keeping the prongs pressed into the man's back, coolly watching while the man writhed in agony.

The woman didn't even try to stop him. Maybe she wasn't a cop after all. She was totally silent, as if understanding Jack's emotion. Prepared to overlook the punishment he was doling out.

"That first one was for me," Jack said, lifting the prod and shifting it to a more sensitive area. "And this really long one... Well, this one is for my brother."

CHAPTER TWENTY-TWO

Justin pulled his car in front of the hospital entrance, then surprised Nikki by leaning over and brushing her mouth with a tender kiss.

"That doesn't seem professional," she said, peeking around his wide shoulder. "Especially with all the lurking reporters."

"The hero of the city doesn't have to worry." Justin grinned but straightened behind the wheel. "Sgt. Smith is surely grateful. By the way, he wants no part of the reward. Says it's all yours."

Nikki smiled. Jack didn't know it yet, but he was about to receive a healthy influx of cash. Ray Gibson had readily confessed to the Judge's murder, along with countless others. Nikki didn't need Sonja's input to know the man had countless psychological evaluations in his future.

"I'm grateful too," Justin said. "You cleared my case."

Which she supposed, was why Justin was taking twenty-four hours off to do "whatever she wanted."

"I took the liberty of packing your bag," he added, "so we could save time. Leave directly from here."

"Where are we going?" she asked, trying to inject some interest in her voice. There were a lot of activities they both enjoyed: the racetrack, a horseback ride, or even a visit to the shooting range. But choosing required too much energy and she was relieved he'd taken over. Besides, she didn't care.

She just wanted a chance to decompress: to forget the sights and smells of Ray's killing farm and those horrible, hungry pigs. "Maybe I just need some sleep," she said. "I feel exhausted."

"It's the crash after the rush, Nik," Justin said, reaching over and squeezing her hand. "A lot happened. Makes it hard to think. So I'm taking you away for the night."

She gave a little nod. But her smile slipped. She wasn't keen for a night at a hotel, even a luxurious one, or the drawn-out rituals of an impersonal restaurant. She just wanted to be somewhere quiet and safe. And to know that the man she loved was safe too.

And she ached to wrap her arms around Gunner's neck and laugh and cry, and let his solid presence soothe her jumbled emotions. But she didn't want to disappoint Justin. He'd already guided her through the countless police interviews and had worked hard to keep the media at bay.

"So I thought we'd drive down so you could be with your favorite guy," Justin was saying. "They've already agreed to let Gunner sit outside with you. We can have beer and wine and dog treats delivered and know that everything is right in our world."

It took a moment for his words to sink in. Then she shot forward and wrapped her arms around his neck. "That sounds perfect," she said, pressing a heartfelt kiss on his cheek, no longer caring who saw.

She never should have doubted Justin. He always knew exactly what she needed, before she knew herself.

"I'll hurry inside," she said, suddenly invigorated. "See the Tanners and be out in half an hour, tops."

Still grinning, she rushed from the car and bounced into the hospital foyer. She hurried toward the elevator, passing a coffee machine and an automated news vendor. Bold headlines proclaimed a missing teen had been saved from a serial killer although full details weren't yet available.

Her steps lightened even further. This was about as good as it could get. Billy was safe, exhausted but alive, and from his grandmother's accounts, even smiling.

"Hey, super sleuth."

Nikki turned toward the familiar voice. Sgt. Lara McCullough strode toward her.

"I just saw Smitty," Lara said, reaching out and pumping Nikki's hand. "They wouldn't let me stay long. Thank you for getting there in time—you know..."

She paused, taking a deep breath. "But Smitty's head is like concrete. He'll be okay. He's beating himself up though, about not noticing Gibson."

Serial killers are hard to recognize, Nikki thought. That's why they were so successful. And she'd been lucky. Driving down that lonely road, spotting Smitty's truck and best of all, having Sparky catch Billy's scent.

"At least you didn't have to shoot Gibson," Lara said. "Apparently he's cooperating. That will give the other families some closure."

"Jack was a big help," Nikki said. "He helped subdue him."

"I heard he got some jabs in." Lara gave an approving nod. "He's quite a kid. Both boys are. We're going to make sure Billy has a part-time job, and Jack too if he wants. Smitty would be delighted if you'd drop by some day when he's feeling better, so he can personally thank you. Better still, visit us at the barn."

Lara moved a little closer, her voice lowering. "If you ever need anything, if we can ever help, just let us know, okay?"

Nikki gave a grateful nod and stepped on the elevator. With her widening police contacts, she'd be assured of seeing the report on Gibson's mental assessment. His eyes haunted her, the intent way he'd stalked her with that chainsaw. Investigators were already in the process of gathering DNA from his farm. Preliminary numbers estimated at least thirty victims although Gibson claimed forty-two wrongdoers had "successfully" repented.

The elevator eased to a stop and she stepped off, turning right on the eighth floor then following the signs. Billy's room was the last one at the end of the sterile corridor. Although the Tanners had no medical insurance, authorities had arranged for a private room. Mrs. Tanner reported Billy had been delighted to have his own television but was too exhausted to take much advantage.

The door was open. Mrs. Tanner spotted Nikki in the doorway and immediately lurched from her chair, fumbling for her cane.

"Come in," she called. "I'm so glad you came."

Nikki grinned—at Billy, at Jack, at Mrs. Tanner. For a moment she couldn't speak. It was cathartic to see Billy safe in a hospital bed, his back wrapped in a clean white dressing, instead of naked, and caged in an execution cell. He looked wan and thin but his smile sparkled, and the sheer gratitude in his eyes spoke volumes.

Jack rose and gave Nikki a fist pump, then surprised her by pulling out an empty chair, positioning it in the prime spot next to Billy's bed.

"Billy was just saying he thought you were too pretty to be a cop," Jack said, shooting his brother a teasing grin.

"And that he was afraid you'd be too nice to pull the trigger," Mrs. Tanner added.

Nikki smiled at a blushing Billy. "I was hoping not to shoot," she admitted. "Luckily your brother didn't listen to my instructions. And he was pretty crafty about sneaking around the barn."

She pretended to frown but it had actually been fortunate that Jack had chosen to follow instead of waiting by the car. And so lucky the dog had bolted up the driveway in search of Billy. A few more minutes... She hid her shiver. It had all turned out—this time.

Everyone was silent for a moment. Then conversation bubbled again and there were no more references to the horrors of the pig farm, just a reunited family sharing their joy. Billy and Jack even argued over whose turn it was to weed the garden, considering that Billy had missed more than a week of chores. Still, it was obvious that the brothers were extremely close.

"Stop bickering, boys." Mrs. Tanner frowned at her grandsons then turned to Nikki. "Would you like something to eat? We have so much food. Sgt. Smitty sent a fruit basket, the police station sent a sandwich tray, and there's even candy from a perfect stranger. Billy will be fattened up in no time and ready to be punished for putting us through this."

Billy stopped arguing with his brother and twisted his head against the pillow. "Are you mad at me, Gran?"

"For taking Jack's place?" Mrs. Tanner sighed. "I raised you boys to look out for each other. So I guess I can't be too angry."

"It's not just that." Billy smiled, so teasingly it was hard to remember that only two days ago he'd been imprisoned in a stall. "Jack said you made a fresh batch of biscuits this morning. But you didn't bring any to the hospital."

Mrs. Tanner hesitated for a moment, an uncharacteristic pause for such a forthright woman. She fiddled with her cane, positioning it carefully beside her chair. And when she finally folded her arms and looked up, her eyes gleamed with unshed tears.

"There aren't any left to bring," she admitted. "I gave them all to Sparky."

OTHER BOOKS BY BEV PETTERSEN

Jockeys and Jewels
Color My Horse
Fillies and Females
Thoroughbreds and Trailer Trash
Studs and Stilettos
Millionaire's Shot
Riding For Redemption
A Scandalous Husband
Backstretch Baby
Shadows of the Mountain
Along Came A Cowboy
Grave Instinct (K9 Mystery)
A Pony For Christmas (Novella)

About the Author

USA Today Bestselling Author Bev Pettersen is a three-time nominee in the National Readers Choice Award and a two-time finalist in RWA's Golden Heart® Contest. She is also the winner of many other international awards including the Reader Views Reviewer's Choice Award, Aspen Gold Reader's Choice Award, Write Touch Readers' Award, a Kirkus Recommended Read, and a HOLT Medallion Award of Merit. She competed for five years on the Alberta Thoroughbred race circuit and is an Equestrian Canada certified coach.

Bev lives in Nova Scotia with her family—humans and four-legged—and when she's not writing novels, she's riding. If you'd like to know about special offers or when her next book will be available, please visit her at http://www.BevPettersen.com where you can sign up for a newsletter.

Made in the USA
Coppell, TX
29 May 2021